Attar of Roses

To my parents,
to my sons,
Tahir, Nasir, and Qasim,
and to Zafar

Attar of Roses
and Other Stories
of Pakistan

Tahira Naqvi

A THREE CONTINENTS BOOK
LYNNE RIENNER PUBLISHERS
BOULDER & LONDON

A Three Continents Book

Published in the United States of America in 1997 by
Lynne Rienner Publishers, Inc.
1800 30th Street, Boulder, Colorado 80301

and in the United Kingdom by
Lynne Rienner Publishers, Inc.
3 Henrietta Street, Covent Garden, London WC2E 8LU

Library of Congress Cataloging-in-Publication Data
Naqvi, Tahira.
    Attar of roses and other stories of Pakistan / Tahira Naqvi.
    p. cm.
    ISBN 0-89410-808-5 (hc :   alk. paper).
    ISBN 0-89410-809-3 (pb :   alk. paper)
    I. Title.
    PR9540.9.N37A94   1997
    813'.54—dc21   97-15869
                                      CIP

British Cataloguing in Publication Data
A Cataloguing in Publication record for this book
is available from the British Library.

Printed and bound in the United States of America

5 4 3 2 1

Contents

⤙⧫ Love in an Election Year ⧫⤚

Benazir Bhutto has a notion she will win. The *mullahs*, their hands lifted ominously, their eyes glinting passionately, are up in arms because,
as they see it, a woman cannot, and if they can help it, will not, hold
executive office. There are pictures in every newspaper. Pronounce-
ments are inked everywhere. But the gaunt-looking young woman with
large piercing eyes and dark sweeping eyebrows seems determined to
become our next Prime Minister. She reminds me of another woman
who had, in a similarly brazen move, wished to be the president of the
country her brother had helped found. That was many years ago. That
winter, I was only fifteen and the *mullahs* hadn't been given a voice
yet.

Winter in Lahore was one's reward for having suffered through
summer and surviving the ordeal. Friendly sunshine offering warm,
tantalizing embraces; a furtive chill in the evening lurking in the darkness, never threatening; plump, tangy tangerines that looked like balls
of pure gold; afternoons of story-telling after school on the veranda
where the bricks on the floor lit up with terra-cotta lights when the
sharp, bright sun filtered through the holes in the latticed balcony; and
Baji Sughra. Baji Sughra was in love in the winter of that year and I was
her confidant and ally. Since she was twenty-one and I only fifteen, I
had to call her *baji*, but the years between us were a mere technicality;
we were friends. And it wasn't that we had become friends overnight,
we had always been good friends, the way most cousins are. Even when
she and her family left for Multan and were gone for three years, we
knew that as soon as we met again it would be as if we had not been
away from each other. That's how it was with cousins—they were
always there.

Within an hour of her arrival from Multan we were chattering
without pause like two myna birds. Uncle Amin had been transferred to
Lahore again, and until their bungalow in Mayo Gardens was ready Baji

1

was to stay with us. Although I tried not to show it, I was amazed, no, overwhelmed, at the change I saw in her. As if by magic, by some process I had no wit to fathom, she appeared so beautiful. Like a sultry actress in an Indian film, like a model in a magazine ad for Pond's Cold Cream. Her hair, which used to hang limply on either side of her face in thick disheveled braids, was now neatly pulled back and knotted with a colorful *paranda* into a long braid down her back, while little wisps danced on her wide, shiny forehead with wild abandon. She also smiled constantly, as if something were making her happy all the time, as if there were some joke she kept remembering, again and again. Her lips, which were once perpetually chapped and sallow, like mine, seemed fuller and soft. I could have sworn she was wearing pink lipstick, except that Auntie Kubra, her mother, would have killed her if she had. Lipstick was for secret dramas enacted in your room when the adults were having their conferences, or for when you were married. I think there was something the matter with her eyes as well. They glimmered as if there were secret lights in them. As for the lashes, they were thicker and sootier than I remembered, while her eyebrows, without a doubt, were longer and darker. Later that day, when I found myself alone for a while in the bedroom I shared with my younger sister and now with Baji Sughra, I examined my own face closely in the dressing table mirror. Front, the sides, then three-quarter angles. Sadly, nothing I saw in the mirror was changed.

At first Baji and I cleared dust from old business. Cousin Hashim had run away from home twice, Aunt S. was pregnant with her first baby, Meena was to become engaged to Hashim's older brother who was in medical school, and Aunt A.'s cold-blooded, unrelenting mother-in-law was a witch whom we would have all liked to see tortured, if not killed. I had seen *Awara*, the latest Nargis-Raj Kapoor film, and we, at our house, were all rooting for Fatima Jinnah, who was running against President Ayub Khan in the 1965 elections. As for the news about Multan, it was skimpy at first. Baji Sughra said the weather was dusty and hot as always, but she had made new friends in school, the mangoes in summer were sweeter and plumper than anywhere else, and yes, she too was rooting for Fatima Jinnah.

"A woman president for Pakistan. Can you believe it Shabo? And she's running against a general too. But she's so like her brother Jinnah, how can anyone not vote for her! She'll win." Baji Sughra looked even more beautiful when she was excited. I wanted to ask her why she was surprised we might have a woman president; sometimes the finer points of politics eluded me. But I knew she had something important to tell me, so I let the query pass.

And finally, when the sun had settled beyond the veranda wall and we had been talking for nearly an hour, she broke the news to me. She was in love. With Javed Bhai, another cousin, a Multan cousin. If I had done my calculations correctly, he was three years older than she was, twenty-three. In his second year at the Engineering University in Lahore, he was one of our cleverest cousins, the one who showed the most promise, the elders had been heard to proclaim. On a visit to his parents' house in Multan, he and Baji Sughra met. It was at one of those family gatherings when the adults are too absorbed in conversation to keep an eye on what the children are doing, or even know where they are. Suddenly Baji and Javed, who weren't strangers and had known each other since childhood, felt they were more than just cousins. This rather overpowering revelation led to secret trysts on the roof of Baji Sughra's house while everyone was taking afternoon naps. Promises were extracted and plans made. Later, after he returned to Lahore, Baji wrote to him, but he couldn't write back for obvious reasons, she explained. I didn't ask her to elaborate; if the reasons were so obvious they would reveal themselves to me sooner or later.

"We'll be married when Javed gets his degree," Baji Sughra informed me with her dimpled smile. "In two years."

I knew Javed Bhai well. He came to our house frequently as did other cousins, especially when they were visiting Lahore from elsewhere, or were students away from home, as Javed Bhai was. He was good-looking, tall, fair-skinned, with a windblown mop of hair, a few locks hanging carelessly over his broad forehead. A thick, black mustache jealously hugged his lips so you didn't see much of them ever. And what a voice he had! He sang film songs in a way that made you feel nervous and mysteriously elated all at the same time. He sang willingly, so we didn't have to beg and beg as we had to do with some of our coy female cousins with good voices, like Meena, for instance.

There was no reason to be amazed at what had happened. Baji Sughra and Javed were like Nargis and Raj Kapoor, like Madhubala and Dilip Kumar. They belonged together. I began to envision Baji Sughra as a bashful bride, weighted down with heavy gold jewelry, swathed and veiled in lustrous red brocade and garlands of roses and cambeli.

"He'll come to see me, Shabo, so you have to help." Baji Sughra held both my hands in hers.

"What can I do?" I said, excitement at the thought of secretly helping lovers rising to form a knot in my throat. "How can I help?" I repeated hoarsely.

"We'll be in your room upstairs and you just keep watch, make sure no one comes up while we're there . . . er . . . talking."

"But what if someone does, what will I say, and . . ." I couldn't continue because all of a sudden I realized this wasn't going to be easy. I had to think. Baji Sughra and I had to make plans.

"Shabo, you have to promise you won't tell anyone about this, not even Meena, not even Roohi, promise." Baji Sughra looked at me as if she were a wounded animal, and I a hunter poised with an arrow to pierce her throat. Her eyes filled with tears. I put my arms around her.

"I promise I won't, I won't tell, Baji, please believe me, I won't." I hugged her, feeling older than my fifteen years, imbued with a sense of importance I had never experienced before. Perhaps that is how Fatima Jinnah feels, I told myself, empowered and bold, ready to take on not only a general but the whole world.

The rendezvous went smoothly. After lunch my parents, Auntie Kubra, and Baji's father Uncle Amin, left to go to our grandparents' room for their usual talks. I couldn't understand how their store of topics for discussion was never depleted. There was so much to say all the time. Politics, family quibbles, who was being absolutely, ruthlessly mean to whom, and who should marry whom and when. Well, finding ourselves alone, Salim (another cousin who had come with Javed Bhai that day, as adviser and helpmate, no doubt), Baji Sughra, my sister Roohi, and I, all took up Javed's suggestion that we play carom.

Four people can play at one time, so we selected partners and found we had one person left over—Roohi. She was the youngest in our group and hadn't quite grasped the intricacies of carom strategy as yet.

"No, no, Roohi can play," Baji hastily intervened when I tried to coax Roohi into observing first and playing later. "She can be your partner, Shabo. I'm going up to finish putting the lace on my *dupatta*. I'll be back soon and then Roohi can be my partner and Salim can watch." Baji had instructed me that I was not to act surprised; assuming a rather nonchalant tone I was to say, "All right, but hurry up," which I did.

"Yes, I will, I only have one side of the *dupatta* to do." She left quickly.

All of us sat down at the carom table which always remained in the same place on the veranda, right across from the windy gully separating the veranda's east and west sections. Even now, when it was cold, we kept the table there, because that was also the sunniest spot on the veranda. What was a little gust of bone-chilling wind every now and then when the sun was bright and warm on our faces?

Within minutes we had formed pairs. Quickly and expertly, Javed Bhai sprinkled some talcum powder on the board to make it slippery and slick, and Salim arranged the black and white disks in a circle. A large red disk, called the 'Queen,' resided safely in the center of the circle. The Queen, over-sized and radiant, carried more points than its austere black and white companions.

I got the first turn. Slouching, my eyes narrowed, assuming the posture I had seen Javed and the other boys use, I aimed at and hit the striker, which was white and somewhat bigger in size than the other disks. I watched gleefully as it first hit and then scattered the other disks all over the board's sleek, yellow surface. Soon all the disks were darting frantically across the wooden board; some, under the expert hands of our male partners, fell into the snug, red nets hanging from the corners of the board, disappearing as if they had never been there in the first place. The Queen, everyone's target at one time or another, was waiting calmly for its turn to disappear. Finally Roohi was given the opportunity to 'push' it into the net.

The first game was over so quickly I began to feel apprehensive. How many games could we play? As Salim began rearranging the disks, Javed said, "I'm going to run down for a pack of cigarettes. You people go ahead without me. I'll be back soon."

Of course he was gone a long time. Roohi began to show impatience and said the game was no fun with only three players. She was learning quickly. Salim said, "I think this is better, you can have more disks to hit. Javed was taking them all away from us." Roohi gave him the look children reserve for adults when they think they're being duped. But, finding him placing the disks together with a solemn air, she turned to give me a stare, discovered I was gazing intently at the carom board, and gave up.

"All right, but where's Baji Sughra?" she muttered.

"She's in her room, where else? Now come on, pay attention." I was getting irritated with her. If we had been in a mystery novel, she'd be the unwanted and unexpected interloper, and would have been knocked down senseless by now.

After a second game in which Roohi won because we more or less forced her to, I asked Salim if he would sing for us. He too, like Javed Bhai, had a strong voice and the uncanny ability to imitate Mukesh, my favorite playback singer. He put on his Raj Kapoor smile and nodded.

"Awara hun," (I'm a rogue) he began after pausing solemnly for a few seconds with his eyes closed, his head tilted to one side. Before I knew it, he was also tapping the carom board rhythmically, keeping beat with his long fingers and the heels of his hands as if the carom board were a *tabla*. Roohi sat back slumped and morose since she wasn't into film songs as yet. I could see she was getting more and more restless, and very soon she would offer to go and bring Sughra Baji down from her room.

"Well, what's going on here?" It was Sughra Baji. She silently made an appearance from the back of the gulley so we didn't see her right away. I was too engrossed in Salim's singing to hear her footsteps. "And where's Javed?" she asked boldly, raising her eyebrows inquiringly without looking at any one directly.

"He went to get cigarettes," Roohi said petulantly, "and we can't play anymore with only three people. Why did you take so long?"

Roohi was still grumbling when Javed Bhai reappeared. Within minutes we were engrossed in another game of carom. Roohi won again. After two more games we decided to end the game; the sun had wandered off somewhere and it was getting chilly. I noticed Sughra Baji was flushed, and couldn't stop smiling, while Javed Bhai hummed and hummed. What was that song? They never once glanced at each other, except in the most indifferent, casual manner. Such subterfuge! I was impressed.

⋯⇒◉⇐⋯

We were making streamers to decorate the front door and the areas along the balconies. The paper flags were twelve inches by six inches and the string was about twenty feet long. Aunt A., who was visiting, had cooked flour paste for us to use for the gluing; Cousin Hashim, after having run off a few times from home because of fights with his father over the subject of academic failure, was now staying with us for a few days to allow his father to cool off, and had been entrusted with obtaining twelve dozen tissue-thin paper flags from a stationery shop at the corner of Allama Iqbal and Davis Roads. We were working feverishly so we could have the streamers ready that afternoon. One more day would be needed for everything to dry and elections were only two days away.

Our work wasn't going too well. After all, this was the first time we were making streamers ourselves. The idea was simple; apply the glue

6

to the narrow white strip of the flag, which I had only recently learned represented minorities in Pakistan, attach it to the string, overlap part of the white strip over the string so it came over, and deftly press the two edges together. But our hands were sticky, the tips of our fingers numb and caky from the starchy globs that remained on them and dried. The process was slowed; we weren't going from one flag to the next as fast as was necessary to meet our deadline.

There was no shortage of help. Aunt A. kept the glue coming, and when Abba came back from work in the afternoon, he too got his hands dirty stringing up flags. All this time Dadima and Dadajan watched us closely, she from her place inside the quilt, he from his easy chair, gurgling his massive, copper-based *hukkah*, occasionally twirling the ends of his large, white mustache between draws. Amma, meanwhile, was concerned mainly with how much mess we were making, and with the possibility that we might come to supper without washing our hands thoroughly first.

Suddenly, around three, there was a noise at the front door and I was surprised to see Auntie Kubra and her husband walk in with Baji Sughra in tow. They moved to their bungalow in Mayo Gardens only a week ago, so why were they here today? True it was Sunday, and anyone could be expected to drop in for a visit. But I started like a guilty thief. I suppose scheming in secret makes you nervous. However, I was relieved to see Baji Sughra not worried at all and smiling. Soon I forgot my discomfort. When she joined us on the floor and told me to start handing her the flags one by one, began slapping glue on the flags with alacrity, handed them to Hashim so he could affix them to the string, I realized we had set up an effective assembly line. Now we were really moving with speed. We were having so much fun I even forgot Javed Bhai.

Then, just as we had almost ten feet of string ready and only ten more to go, Baji's parents, Abba, Amma, and our grandparents trooped out of there, one by one. They were heading for the room we used as dining room and living room, which meant they were going to have tea and a conference. I didn't like the way they all went in together. If it was a dialogue about Fatima Jinnah's future they were planning, they would have stayed on the veranda and conducted the discussion right here. Allah Rakha, the houseboy, would have brought tea and *samosas* on a tray, and he would have also refreshed Dadajan's *hukkah* with fresh water and more coals. Obviously the elders had in mind some other topic, not suitable for our ears. Once again I was gripped by the same feeling of dread that first assailed me when I saw Sughra Baji's parents walk into our house this afternoon.

Cousin Hashim, perhaps anxious to run out for a quick cigarette, suggested we take a break. Roohi, her frock front soiled with a combination of glue and dirt, agreed. Sughra Baji said she had a whole batch of the party's pins for us, so we took the unfinished streamer up on the parapet to dry, and washed our hands. The pins were small, but the lantern, Fatima Jinnah's emblem, was clearly visible in all its detail. I had thought it odd that General Ayub's emblem should be the rose. A military dictator had little use for flowers. A sword perhaps, or a cannon would have been a more appropriate symbol for his party.

"He's just trying to look benevolent, show people how gentle he is, how harmless, but it's just a front," Sughra Baji explained when I took my puzzlement to her. "But you see why the lantern is important? It's a symbol of light, of enlightenment. Also, the lantern is a poor man's source of light, so there are social implications too." Sometimes Baji Sughra forgot I was so much younger than she and said things I did not grasp easily. But happy in the thought that she trusted my intelligence to address such complex matters to me, I often pretended to comprehend more than I actually did.

The streamer went up the next day with the joint endeavors of Cousin Hashim and Allah Rakha. It looked so short and inadequate at first, especially when you compared it to the rows and rows of ready-made flags, colorful banners and streamers that decorated shop fronts and other buildings up and down our road. But after a while we ignored its length. Filled with the satisfaction of having created it all by ourselves, we congratulated each other on a job well-done. Dadajan and Abba went further; they boasted about our endeavors to any one who came to visit. "All done right here, they worked hard," Dadajan told uncles and aunts whose visits were increasing as the day of the elections drew close. We were quite proud of ourselves after all.

Election day came and went. All night, as the votes were being counted, we stayed up. Even Dadima, who usually couldn't keep her eyes open after ten, huddled in her quilt, awake late into the night, listening to songs, dramas, news bulletins, vote-counts. Roohi, stubbornly fighting sleep, was curled up under Dadima's quilt. We gathered around Dadajan's Philips radio, a small, plain-looking, unpretentious box on the surface, but of such immense import this night, holding so much excitement. Rounds of tea for the grownups were followed by milk and Ovaltine for Roohi and myself, and Cousin Hashim, in deference to his green stubble I suppose, and because he was a guest, was offered tea instead. Aunt A. had made thick, granular carrot *halwa* for the occasion, and there were bags of roasted, unshelled peanuts for all of us.

⟶═◉═◄⟵

Fatima Jinnah lost the election. The voting was rigged in such clever and inventive ways that no one could prove it had actually happened, or how. There was a picture of her in the newspaper the next morning in which she looked sadder than any tragic heroine in any movie I had ever seen. She seemed to have aged twenty years. Her face had crumpled in one night, and in her eyes was an empty, faraway look. This is how Jinnah, her brother, must have looked as he lay dying, I thought, from a disease no one could cure.

Celebrations in the streets consisted of cars tooting their horns, tongas hitched with loudspeakers blaring away film songs and war songs, anthems about soldiers surrendering their lives for the motherland, paeans reeking of patriotic fervor. Young men on motorbikes, obviously elated by the victory of the handsome general, raced down the road in front of our house, in both directions, recklessly and dangerously weaving in and out of traffic that was frantic enough on ordinary days, and was tumultuous this morning.

A pall hung over our house. Dadajan had begun by cursing heavily, calling Ayub Khan names that made our ears burn, and then had lapsed into unhappy grunts as he rummaged through the things on his desk, going through the contents of his drawers as if he had lost something important. Dadima continued to mutter, "She had no chance, the poor woman, no chance to begin with, ahh . . ."

Amma and Abba put up stoical fronts and went about their business with long faces and deep sighs, but no harsh words. As for me, I had a sinking feeling in my stomach, the sort of feeling one experiences after poor marks on a test or a disparaging remark from one's favorite teacher. I also wanted to take a club to General Ayub's head. Our sweeperess, Jamadarni, proclaimed angrily, waving her straw *jharu* before her like a baton, "Someone should go and pull his mustache, the dog!" Roohi, a little overwhelmed by the expression of grief she saw around her, burst into tears. Cousin Hashim was restrained with great difficulty by Allah Rakha as he threatened to go out and cuff the man who was attempting to break into two a large, cardboard lantern that had adorned the entrance of the little tea shop right next to our front door. And so we mourned.

That evening Baji Sughra came to visit us with her parents. She wore a sad look, and seeing her face so pale and her eyes wet with unshed tears I thought how beautiful she was when saddened. I also envied her. She was feeling the same emotion I was, but she could feel more deeply than I and that's why there were tears in her eyes. She wanted to go upstairs, so after the preliminary *salaams* and declarations about what a terrible thing had happened, and may God curse Ayub Khan, etc., etc., she and I slipped away, leaving the adults to their intricately philosophical analysis of Fatima Jinnah's crushing defeat.

No sooner had we entered my room than Baji Sughra fell on the bed and began sobbing. I was startled by this unexpected show of emotion and then, because I wasn't altogether stupid, I realized her anguish had its origin in something other than Fatima Jinnah's failure to rise to the leadership of our country.

"What's the matter, Baji?" I bent over her prostrate form anxiously. "What's happened?" In my head, like words from a screenplay, a voice whispered warnings about love gone awry, my heart knocked against my ribs as if ready to jump out of there.

"Oh Shabo, my life is finished, I'm going to die," she said brokenly. "Abba and Amma have arranged a match for me, they had been making plans all this time and I didn't know. They don't like Javed, Amma said it would be a long time before he was ready for marriage, ohhh . . . what am I going to do?" She covered her face with her hands, flung her head down on her knees and wept as if her heart were breaking.

I was stunned. This was just like in the movies. Cruel society and equally cruel fate.

Taqdeer ka shikwah kaun kare   Who can complain about destiny
Ro ro ke guzara karte hain.   I spend my life crying

Lata's soulful voice ambled into my head so clearly I could even trace the musical notes. Ahh, poor Baji!

"But did you explain? Did you tell Auntie you love him and you can't marry anyone else?" I shook her arm.

"Yes, yes, but Amma said this was just foolishness, oh Shabo, she doesn't care about my feelings, no one does, and neither Amma nor

Abba like Javed . . . I'll kill myself if they force me to marry someone else." Sughra Baji wailed.

"But why don't they like Javed?" How could anyone not like Javed?

"He's too young, he has no means of supporting a wife as yet, such nonsense! And that bastard they've found for me, he's a businessman, he has a big house, he has a car, oh Shabo they think he's perfect. But how can I marry him? What about Javed?" A new wave of anguish swept over her; she smacked her head with her fists.

Frightened by her despair I said, "Maybe we should talk to Dadima, she's the only one who can help, and she'll talk to Dadajan and no one can go against his wishes." Suddenly I felt better. Dadima had come to my aid in moments of crisis many a time, and her influence over Dadajan was indubitable.

"They've already talked, they've discussed everything and Dadajan has given his approval. Oh Shabo, my life is over, I'll kill myself, I'll be a corpse instead of a bride, they'll see."

"Don't talk like that Baji," I said fearfully, visions of her dressed in her bridal garb and laid out like a corpse careening madly in my head. "There must be something we could do."

"What? What can we do?" she asked, looking at me with pleading eyes.

"What about Javed Bhai? Why doesn't he come and beg, why doesn't he tell Auntie and Uncle that he loves you and he'll take good care of you and . . ." I realized how foolish my words must sound. If we were in the movies Baji Sughra would have indeed killed herself by taking poison which someone like me would have supplied to her, or she would have run away at the last minute, just as the *maulavi sahib* was getting ready in the other room to conduct the *nikah*. But this wasn't the movies, alas. And I was in no position to supply poison or any other form of assistance. All I could manage was unhappiness and tears. It didn't amaze me that in the space of one day I had experienced the urge to take the club to the heads of two men.

⋅⇒◉⇐⋅

The wedding was grand. No one expected it to be anything less. Auntie Kubra and her husband had a very large circle of Railway friends and our aunts, uncles, cousins, and second-cousins didn't come in small numbers either. Also, this was the first wedding in Auntie Kubra's family. Baji Sughra's dowry was overwhelming. Thirty suits, nearly all richly

11

filigreed and embroidered with golden thread, five sets of jewelry, furniture, carpets, cutlery, crockery, a television set—the list was endless, I thought enviously.

Baji Sughra cried continuously, but only in front of me and our cousin Meena. She didn't want to distress her parents; they had enough on their hands already, and sending off a daughter is cause enough for sorrow, although joy has its place too on such occasions. Baji Sughra's tears went unnoticed. A sad bride is traditional, so that if anyone saw her in tears the only conclusion drawn was that the poor girl was weeping at the thought of leaving her parents' home. In fact, if you showed too much excitement at your wedding, you'd be accused of immodesty.

One evening, soon after all of Baji's friends and female cousins had finished applying *ubtan*, that foul-smelling turmeric paste which was supposed to make her skin glow for her husband, to her legs, feet, hands and face, she gestured for me to follow her into the bathroom.

"This is for Javed," she whispered when we were alone, handing me an envelope. "You'll see him in a few days I'm sure, please give it to him. You'll take good care of it, Shabo, won't you? If it falls into the wrong hands, I'll be ruined." She sniffled.

"Of course I'll take good care of it Baji, don't worry." I couldn't bear to see her so sorrowful. My heart was wrenched at the thought of this tragedy. I hated tragedies. When I started reading a new novel, I'd check the ending first just to make sure it wasn't a tragedy. If it were, I didn't bother to read the book. Why waste your time with dead ends? But this was different, I told myself confidently. There was hope here.

In the days I waited to see Javed Bhai, the letter secure in my possession, I began listening to sad songs on the radio. Lata's melancholy melodies and the singer Talat Mehmud's sad laments drenched my spirits until I felt as if I were a part of Baji Sughra, a small, hidden component of her self. I even dreamt about Javed. In one disturbing dream he clasped me in his arms and together we ran across a heath; there was a mist, clouds and then a storm preceded by dark, swirling clouds and I lost him. He reappeared later, and we sat side by side on the veranda where we had played carom, right across the windy gulley, the sunniest spot on the veranda. He sang. In another dream, even more disturbing than the first, I saw Baji Sughra being laid out for burial. But she wasn't wearing the white burial shroud; instead she was dressed in her bridal suit, the gilt-embroidered, heavily filigreed *dupatta* covering her face, the long strands of the gold frill dangling limply from the *dupatta's* edges.

I protected the letter Baji had entrusted to my care with the utmost diligence. Afraid of leaving it in a place where Amma, Roohi or Aunt S. or Aunt A. might accidentally stumble upon it, I carried it in my bra, which was only a size 28 so that at first I had difficulty straightening out the bulge. Finally I found a corner below my armpit which held the epistle snugly. At night I took it out and slipped it under my pillow.

Javed Bhai was a long time in coming. He didn't show up until the night before the wedding. When he came, he brought with him a large basket of oranges for us, saying these had come from his father's orange groves near Multan. He explained to Dadima that he had been instructed to drop them off right away.

He looked like someone who had been living on the streets. A Majnu, the mad lover. His clothes were wrinkled and shabby, his hair tousled and uncombed, there were gaunt hollows in his cheeks, and his eyes were restless. He smiled when Dadima asked him about his parents, and inquired if they were planning to come to the Sughra's wedding, but it was the smile of a man who had received a death sentence.

I slipped him the note, which was badly crushed by now and streaked with sweat, while he was talking to Dadima. She turned to push the heavy *hukkah* closer to her bed, was briefly engaged in a minor tug with the long pipe which had become tangled, and I swiftly transferred the envelope to Javed's hand. I had read the letter many times. Baji had instructed me to memorize the contents in case I had to destroy the missive and was compelled to give Javed her message verbally. The letter was not a coherent piece of writing and consisted of phrases like, "Fate has played a cruel trick on us," "don't forget me," "I was not unfaithful, you'll see," "remember my love," etc., etc. Certainly I would have worded it differently, especially when I knew it was to be a last confession, given it a literary twist, for after all, who knew where it might end up. Javed stayed for a few minutes longer afterward and then left. I will always remember the haunted look on his face as he walked out the front door.

The next day the *nikah* ceremony took place around four in the afternoon. The *maulavi sahib* asked Sughra Baji if she would agree to marry Salman Ali, son of Numan Ali with a *mehr* of fifty thousand rupees to be paid to her when she requested. You're not supposed to exceed the bounds of modesty and respond enthusiastically with a 'yes' right away; all brides must wait until the query is repeated for the third and last time and then, after a reasonable pause, come out with a demure 'Hmm.'

I was seized with a horrible thought. Was Baji Sughra planning to say 'no' in the presence of the *maulavi sahib*, the two uncles who were acting as witnesses, her own father? In one movie at least, I had seen a bride take to such recklessness. The huddled form swaddled in red and yellow *dupattas* was still. Oh God! What was going to happen now? My heart raced. *Maulavi sahib* was getting ready to present the question for the third time. The Koranic verses poured effortlessly from his mouth while he stroked his beard. Soon he asked, "Do you, Sughra Bano Rehman, agree to marry Salman Ali, son of Numan Ali, for a *mehr* of fifty thousand rupees to be paid upon request?"

One of our aunts, Auntie Najma, who was sitting close to Baji Sughra, patted Baji with one massively ringed, chubby hand. Up and down the hand went, slowly, deliberately. "Come on child, come now, don't be shy, daughter." She smiled with her eyes lowered as she whispered into the place on the *dupatta* behind which Baji's ear might be. There was a slight tremor in the bundle of *dupattas* and then we all heard a sound. It could have been a whimper. A sob. Even a whisper of protest.

"Congratulations!" The *maulavi sahib* said, turning to the men with a self-satisfied smile. Aunt Najma clasped Baji Sughra to her breast and started crying and soon there were cries of 'Congratulations! Congratulations!' everywhere.

Later, as every bride and groom must, Baji Sughra and her groom were sitting together on a sofa while everyone watched them. The bridegroom, contrary to my expectations, was neither short, stocky, nor bald. Most businessmen I knew were. This one, to my dismay, was tall, slim, sported a mustache like Javed Bhai's, and a crop of dark, wavy hair, all of which didn't make it easy for me to hate him. To make matters worse, he kept smiling in a rather delightful way. I felt guilty that I couldn't despise him immediately, and the sense of betrayal grew strong in me as I continued to watch him sitting next to Baji Sughra looking handsome and elegant in his cream-colored *kemkhab sherwani* and white and gold silk turban. Like a prince, I admitted to myself shamelessly.

I forced myself to look away and turned my attention to Baji Sughra. Tears trickled down her smooth, silvery cheeks as if moving along of their own volition. She was so pale and still. Almost as if drained of life. I tried to get close to her, but the crowd of guests, women, young and old and children, especially girls, jostled and crammed and shoved for a place from which to view the bride and groom clearly. There was such laughter and giggling. So much free-floating gaiety. Everyone could dip into it without reserve.

Someone pushed me and I fell, my *dupatta* got tangled with a woman's stiletto heel, and before I could get to my feet and steady myself, Baji and Salman had been engulfed by the fervent throng of wedding guests.

⊶═◉◠═⊰

The *valima*, the reception at the groom's house after the wedding, is an important event. The bride's parents get an opportunity to see their daughter in her new surroundings, shy and reticent still, but happy. However, happy was not a word that came to mind that evening for me. When we arrived at Salman's house my head buzzed with such horrible visions that I had difficulty concentrating on anything. I forgot to carry in Dadima's Kashmiri shawl from the car, left my own sweater with the mother-of-pearl buttons at home, and dropped an earring somewhere which made Amma lose her temper.

I knew Baji hadn't tried to kill herself, or we would have heard about it already and wouldn't be coming to attend the *valima*. But there were other possibilities I had entertained all night. She tells her husband the truth, thereby incurring his wrath; she tells him nothing but remains cold to his affections, thereby incurring his displeasure; she offers him her body but keeps her soul from him and he guesses there's something wrong and turns from her, rejects her in private, maintaining a subterfuge for the world in public.

We arrived to find Baji Sughra sitting on a bright red sofa, surrounded as every bride is fated, by women and girls. She was wearing a pink tissue *gharara* embroidered heavily with golden thread and sequins. The *dupatta*, this evening, only partially covered her face and her hair had been swept back from her forehead, perhaps braided with a golden *paranda* and threaded cambeli buds. She looked lovely, like a fairy princess on a throne. I went up to her. At first she didn't see me because her head was lowered. I touched her hand.

"*Salaamalekum* Baji," I whispered.

She immediately turned to me, and we hugged. I felt a lump in my throat, my eyes misted. As we embraced, the sharp gold edges of her long *kundan* earrings cut into my cheek. I looked at her face. Her skin was as pink as the pink of her clothes, her eyes were luminous, as if lit from within, her lips opened shyly in a smile.

15

"Shabo, my dear Shabo, how are you? I've been waiting for you."

"I'm fine," I said. "I gave your letter . . ." I began.

"Shhh . . ." she cut me off urgently, "we'll talk about that later."

"So, are you happy?" I asked, a bitter note creeping into my voice as if she'd wounded my feelings.

"Yes Shabo, I am happy. Salman is such a wonderful man, he's so nice." She spoke coyly.

Nice? What had happened to her? What was she saying? Nice? What about Javed? I wanted to ask her.

"There's something you must do for me," she whispered when we were alone for a few minutes during dinner. "You must get my letter back for me."

"What?" My heart lurched. I felt as if she had slapped me. "But Javed Bhai . . ." I tried to say, my eyes fixed on her face, her beautiful pink face.

"Shhh, please Shabo dearest, just get it back, will you, please?"

"But why? And how . . ."

"Oh, you're such a baby Shabo, how can I tell you anything, you don't understand, do you? Please, my dear little sister, just do this last favor for me." She held my hands in hers and for a moment I could have sworn I saw tears floating in her eyes. But it might have been an illusion created by the bright overhead lights in the drawing room and the dark *kajal* she wore in her eyes that evening.

I didn't appreciate being called a baby, and I wasn't keen on bringing the letter back to her. If I had any courage I'd have told her to do it herself. I was no longer her friend and ally, I'd have said. Anyway, even if I tried, I couldn't force Javed to return the letter.

"All right," I said helplessly when she began to sniffle, and patted her small, thin, heavily ringed hand.

Of course, Javed Bhai refused to give the letter back. He cursed the whole world and said unkind things about Baji.

"She's false, inconstant, taken in by the highest bidder, so easily sold." His words sounded like a dialogue from a film. Secretly I agreed with him.

"But Javed Bhai, she couldn't do anything, you know, what could she do?"

"She could have fought, she could have taken a stand, why didn't she?" He stared at me questioningly, but perhaps hit with the realization I was too young to give him a satisfactory answer, he turned away, biting his lips and shaking his head sadly.

"But the letter isn't important any more, why don't you give it back?"

I begged. At first he ignored my pleas. Some moments later he took the letter out of his shirt pocket and angrily tore it into a hundred pieces, his face contorted as his hands worked the letter into shreds. Then he flung the pieces over the parapet. Slowly the tiny scraps flew down and away, this way and that, scattered by the wind like eddying autumn leaves.

-->≡◯⊂≡<-

Time hasn't been very charitable to Baji Sughra. She's fat and dour. Yesterday, while I sat in the drawing room of her large, spacious bungalow and had tea with crispy, spicy samosas, she went on and on in a heavy, unhappy voice about the shortcomings of her female servant, complaining that it had become tiresome finding suitable help these days. Cutting short her impassioned discourse on the subject of female help, I asked her about Benazir Bhutto. Was she rooting for her?

"She's had plastic surgery, you know," raising a plump, ringed hand, Baji Sughra offered in response to my question. "And she's too much in love with that horrible husband of hers, that playboy. She'll never win."

While Baji poured another cup of tea for herself, I thought about Fatima Jinnah. One could say the country at that time was young. That Fatima Jinnah was old and weary. That she reminded people too much of a past that needed to be put aside so the country could move forward unfettered. That democracy was a word with enormously complicated and rather foreign connotations. And so she didn't win.

"As I see it, Shabo, my dear," Baji Sughra continued philosophically, "she just likes to take risks. Why, she's always pregnant. What can she do if she's pregnant?"

"She's not crippled or disabled, Baji, pregnancy is not a debilitating illness." I found myself using a tone of voice I had never used with Baji before.

"Well Shabo, she wants too much. Just think, you can either be a good wife and mother or a good leader. And she wants to be all three. Now, tell me Shabo, is that possible? How is that possible?"

"Do you ever think about Javed Bhai?" I asked.

First published in *Her Mother's Ashes and Other Stories by South Asian Women in Canada and the United States* (Toronto: Toronto South Asian Publications, Spring 1994).

17

→❐ Attar of Roses ❐←

Where has it gone, the life
Once adorned by your tresses?
Entice me not to the abode of the beloved,
My being is wary of the path that leads there.

Hmm . . . hmmm . . . good, Saeed thought. Swiftly he turned some pages. If only he could take the magazine home with him. He scanned the cover—ten rupees. Too much for just one magazine, for one poem. His children would be waiting eagerly for the mangoes he bought every day and a ten-rupee note was all he had this afternoon; it was either the magazine or the mangoes. He wiped his face with a soiled handkerchief that had soaked up the day's sweat and grime and, ignoring the resentful stare of the owner of the book stand, continued reading.

The stand was located in a busy section of Alam Market and he was jostled by passersby as he tried to concentrate on the poem before him. A river of people pressed in all directions with great urgency, everyone hastening to the refuge of darkened rooms and ice water, anxiously seeking reprieve from the glazed, torrid afternoon heat. Sweat ran down his back in little streams. He flapped the back of his shirt to get some air and wiped his face again.

More poems on another page. Here was one he could have written himself. Soon he forgot the crowds, the perspiration that covered his face like a film of oil, the cacophonous din of traffic. The poem, melodic and richly textured, was all that remained. But what was this? Something tugged at his attention, a scent flooded in. Attar of roses? Yes, strong, potent, attar of roses, Saeed told himself, an exciting aroma, easily recognizable. He glanced sideways. To his right was a woman clad in a black *burka* that covered her from the top of her head to her ankles. She was so close to him that if he stretched out his hand he could have touched the satiny black linen of her covering. With her back to him, she riffled through a pile of magazines and as she moved his gaze fell upon her hands. Never had he seen hands of such extraordinary beauty. The skin was pale and unlined, the color a pearly shade of jasmine, the fingers slender, the nails neatly rounded and pink, and the little he saw of the wrist was encased in black glass bangles that made a silvery, tinkling sound every time she moved her arm. On the back of her hand the thin blue veins were like delicate shadows across the face of a rose petal. He had not seen such a hand before! How yielding to the touch, he thought, the clasp like a promise of love. And then, as his eyes followed her slim form down to where the *burka* ended at the level of her ankles, he saw her feet. Wrapped in dark sandals with narrow leather bands, they were like the moon at midnight, gray clouds rolling in thin strips across a disc of gold.

Saeed realized he was staring at her, although she didn't seem to be aware of his scrutiny for she remained engrossed in the magazines. His behavior was improper, he looked away quickly. But within moments his attention was drawn to her again. She had lifted a corner of her veil and was now talking to the owner of the book stand, something about the price, he overheard. Because her back was to him he didn't see any part of her face, not even a cheek or a brow. While he looked on, his heart hammering in his chest as if he were a love-sick schoolboy, she took some money from a purse that hung on her arm and handed it to the vendor.

She was going to walk away soon. She would disappear into the crowds that were milling about them and he would never see her again. He could not let her go. If only she had lifted her veil and looked in his direction; he had to see her face. Saeed felt anxiety rise in him like a dry cough, panic gripped him, he felt as if he were in a boat deluged with water, about to go down, about to sink. What could he do?

A tiny voice of remonstrance whispered in his brain, but a louder voice clamored in his ears like a trumpet, and he couldn't shut it out. *Follow her,* the voice screamed gratingly, cutting into his heart.

Holding the magazine she had just purchased in one hand, she adjusted her veil with the other and stepped in the direction of the fruit-seller. Like a man under a spell, made stupid by some power he did not know, Saeed dropped his magazine on the rack and blindly took a few steps after her. As he did so he collided with an elderly man who rolled his eyes angrily and muttered an admonition.

"Why don't you look where you're going, sir!"

The man's harsh tone jolted Saeed out of his dazed state. All at once he was seized with an overpowering sense of shame and guilt. What was he doing? He was an educated school-master who attempted every day to instill in his students the moral and ethical values of his society. How could he have considered pursuing a strange woman merely in order to satisfy a foolish, impulsive whim? He was overcome by a surge of mortification, his heart beat violently. Had anyone noticed his peculiar behavior? he wondered uneasily. Surely the book-seller had observed his actions. He turned around and raced to the bus stop across the road.

--≒◎≒--

While Saeed stood outside his house waiting for his wife to open the door, he suddenly remembered that he had forgotten to buy the mangoes. It was his custom to bring home some fruit every day. The children would be disappointed, and he would have to make up some excuse to his wife for not having any fruit with him today. He heard her struggling with the latch on the other side of the door, and the words leaped out of his mouth before the door was fully ajar.

"The mangoes didn't look good today, I'm sure they weren't ripe, I didn't buy any."

His wife, Razia, appeared to be startled by the urgency in his tone. She mumbled something about the heat and that he might have picked up melons instead. He almost ran past her, dropping his bag on a *charpai* in the courtyard along the way before heading for the bathroom.

Two large brass containers filled with water stood in a corner of the small room he and his family used for washing and bathing only. Bending down, Saeed scooped up water in his cupped hands and splashed it on his face repeatedly. There was a fire in his head he couldn't extinguish, his skin burned. He came out without drying himself, water dripping profusely from his face and hair, trickling down onto his shirt, blending with his sweat.

The children, exhausted from the long morning in school, their energy drained from them like a river sapped from its bed, were already asleep on a rope cot set against the wall. Saeed sat down on a *charpai* not far from them and waited for Razia to bring in his lunch. He could hear the clatter of pans in the kitchen, and the smell of kerosene filled his nostrils as she started up the stove. Brushing back moist strands of hair from his forehead, he closed his eyes. The bedroom was like a furnace. The ceiling fan whirred noisily, sending down waves of hot and humid air. The bedsheet under Saeed had the effect of a hot water bottle. He shifted around for a cool spot, but he knew he would find none.

Razia brought his food on a tray and put it down on the bed before him. A dish of spicy, stewed potatoes and peas, a bowl of *daal*, fluffy *rotis*, and a tall glass of chilled *lassi*. He attacked the food furiously.

"So hot, it's so hot," Razia grumbled. Sweat poured from her face and neck, tiny wisps of wet hair clung to her forehead, and her eyes drooped. She lay down on the cot next to his, sighed a few times, pulled back her hair, threw it over the edge of the rope cot away from her face and her neck, and shut her eyes.

As if seeing her for the first time, Saeed stopped eating for a minute and stared at her prostrate form. There were tiny beads of perspiration on her upper lip. Her mouth was sullen, the lips dry and colorless, slightly apart. She looked tired, there were dark rings around her eyes and fine lines crowded the area at the sides of her mouth like tiny cobwebs. A faint odor of sweat, mustard oil, and turmeric emanated from her. The *shalwar* and *kameez* she wore this afternoon were of a flimsy voile, the color dull, green or gray, he couldn't quite make out. There must have been a floral pattern on the fabric at one time, but constant washing had blurred the design, the cloth itself now drab and limp.

Saeed couldn't remember when he had last observed his wife so closely. In moments of intimacy when he clung to her in feverish nighttime passion in the dark, he saw nothing but the throbbing brightness of his own release. He had forgotten what her breasts looked like, or her thighs, or the roundness of her belly.

Gulping down some *lassi* quickly, the taste of sweetened yogurt lingering pleasantly on his tongue, he held the small uneven chunks of ice in his mouth, rolling them around, savoring the coolness before crushing them between his teeth.

During the night heavy clouds rolled in and the morning sky was overcast. The air, Saeed noticed with relief, had a much-needed freshness to it. The city's spirits will be lifted today, he thought. People will break easily into smiles and tell jokes as the clouds thicken again and the downpour begins. Children will dance in the streets, their dark, naked bodies glistening with moisture as they jump up and down impetuously in the summer deluge and splash around in the muddy puddles. The foliage, dust-ridden and stiff, will be washed clean, and the aroma of damp earth will be everywhere.

The rain started when he entered the school compound. He could hear the students' voices rising excitedly to greet the downpour. Some of the younger boys raced across the grounds while others walked with slow deliberation so they could get soaking wet. A few, older, more cautious, watched eagerly from the verandas, their bodies restive with undisguised energy. Saeed's umbrella swished above his head in the torrent as he hurriedly made his way across the school ground to his classroom.

Class 10 was reading the poetry of Iqbal this morning. The boys, who were no longer boys but young men with untidy stubble and downy mustaches and who saw no purpose in studying poetry, especially on a day when rain was coming down so heavily, were edgy. This was a morning for leaping about in the slushy puddles, sitting around with friends, making absentminded prattle and drinking tea, a morning for dirty shoulder-slapping jokes and loud, unchecked laughter. Everything studying Iqbal's poetry was not.

> It is proper that one's heart be guarded by intellect,
> But sometimes let it be alone.

Saeed recited a couplet from one of Iqbal's *ghazals*. "Well, let's analyze this couplet for a minute," he said, leaving his desk to stand near the classroom window from where he could see the rain and hear the thunderous rumblings of the clouds. "Can anyone tell me what the poet means?"

"It means, sir, that although we have a duty to sit in class and listen to you, every now and then we should think about running out into the rain." It was Shabir, smiling boldly, who retorted.

"All right, let's say you're partly correct. Staying in class is an activity dictated by the intellect and getting out of here is an act that is motivated by the heart. But let's go a step further. What does being outside signify?" Saeed looked at the students' faces, wondering if they had any inkling where he was taking them with the question.

"Sir, outside is fun, it's a good time, it's . . . it's what you can't have, maybe shouldn't have?" Navid spoke thoughtfully, nervously rubbing the back of his neck with one hand as he squinted his eyes at his teacher.

"Yes, yes, you're following the proper line of thought, but there's more, there's more."

"Sir, the heart is supposed to make you act irrationally, impulsively, so you have no time to think. One can't always be like that sir, but sometimes one needs a little madness." It was Masud this time, a man-child who had been in love more than once already, was rejected each time, and was now metamorphosed into a poet.

Yes, Saeed contemplated, a little madness, a little passion. As the poet Ghalib had said:

> I'm not content to race in the veins,
> What is blood if it does not spill from the eyes?

While Saeed engaged some of the students in the front of the class in a discussion, those at the back, seeing this as their cue, became talkative. Finally he gave everyone a written assignment.

Returning to his desk Saeed took out his notebook and opened it to the page where his own unfinished *ghazal* was inscribed.

> Those whose caravans have been destroyed
> In the way of adoration and passion,
> What will it serve to tell them . . .

"What will it serve to tell them . . . " Saeed silently repeated the third line several times over. Unable to find an appropriate conclusion to the thought he had generated in the first two lines, he felt as if he were in a labyrinth where every time he turned a corner with the anticipation that now he would find the end waiting for him, he came up against another wall. He tapped his pen on the notebook while mental images of the woman he had seen in the market eroded his concentration.

The day dragged on with interminable slowness. The last period Urdu literature class was taking a test, and as he paced in the aisles between the rows of desks, a feeling of familiar anxiety began gnawing at him. Like his students, he wanted to dart out of the classroom, run blindly through the hundred billowing curtains of rain, keep running until he was drenched to the skin and the fever of the obsession raging in his head had finally cooled down. Chiding himself, as he had been doing often lately, he took out his handkerchief and wiped his face and neck with it; the handkerchief was grimy and damp, the edges curling inward forlornly. He hastily thrust it back into his shirt pocket.

The rain ended suddenly while he was collecting notebooks. Soon waves of humidity would be pressing down again from all sides, and the air would become more stifling now than it had been before the downpour.

⟶⟩◯⟨⟵

From his place at the bus stop Saeed could observe the book stand clearly. The area was crowded as usual. He sauntered over to the sherbet-*wallah's* cart under the shade of a large peepal tree a few feet from the bus stop and bought a glass of chilled, sugary Rooh Afza. The momentary caress of the drink's sweet aromatic coolness offered an immensely satisfying reprieve from the brutal afternoon mugginess. He decided to buy another glassful.

The bus was late, and when it arrived it would be jammed with people. There would be men and boys hanging out of the doorway and, if he was lucky, he might get standing space. Wedged between bodies rank with summer odors, he would suffer for half an hour before he arrived at his destination. The next bus would come around two-thirty. A glance at his watch revealed it was two already. Transferring to the other hand the plastic bag which contained his students's notebooks and his own texts, Saeed wiped his forehead with his shirt sleeve and walked slowly toward the book stand.

He bought a copy of *Nawa-e-Waqt* and while paying the man for the newspaper, he looked around from the corners of his eyes. Several women clad in black *burkas* went by, some coming in from the front, others from behind. How would he know her? He was sure he would. But it wasn't fair that the women were in such a hurry. He needed time for scrutiny, he had to look carefully. Overcome by desperation, his glance darting from hand to hand, he looked fervidly for the feet he knew would be hers. But was this not madness?

Then he spotted her. She was bent over a heap of mangoes on the fruit stand to his right. Her veil lifted with one hand, she picked up mangoes with the other, turning each one around, taking it close to her nose to sniff it before dropping it into the brown paper bag the fruit vendor was patiently holding out for her.

Saeed stuffed the newspaper in his bag and made his way to the fruit stand. The mangoes looked inviting. *Perhaps I can see her face* today, he mused, if only I can see her face. She turned once while he stood fingering mangoes nervously and he thought he caught a glimpse of her eyes for only a second. Dark, circled with kohl, like nights of love, he thought. The fragrance of rose attar seemed to fill his entire being. As if incapable of movement, he stood rooted to the ground, his heart hammering against his ribs in frenetic rhythms.

Picking up a mango, a slim, extremely fragrant variety, he handed it to the fruit seller's assistant, a young boy who had been waiting to help him.

"Weigh four of these," he said, unmindful of the fact that this was the most expensive kind of mango and would cost him at least ten rupees.

While the boy weighed and then placed the mangoes in a paper bag for him, he fumbled in his pocket for money.

"Nine rupees and fifty paisas," Saeed heard the boy say.

She had paid and was preparing to move off.

"The change, *sahib*," the boy said. But Saeed had no time to collect his change. She was going to take the bus, he realized.

It was the two-thirty bus she boarded and as he scrambled in after her he saw her moving toward the women's section in the front of the bus. Soon he was swallowed by a throng of passengers packed together like matchsticks in a matchbox. Saeed could no longer see her. There were *burkas* everywhere.

The pounding of his heart grew until he felt he would collapse on the floor of the bus. He tried to force his way through the crowd of men around him, pushing and jostling as he inched forward. Suddenly the bus stopped. Several people got off, several more came on, women buried in white *chadors* and black *burkas*, hollow-cheeked tired men, sweating and exhausted, children with pale, drawn faces and listless eyes. He craned his neck to see if she was among the passengers who had just alighted. He could not tell.

A weariness descended upon him like a thick blanket, suffocating, weighty. He breathed heavily. The man standing next to him was chewing betel leaf furiously, a dark orange liquid oozing from the corners of his mouth which he occasionally wiped with his hand in a careless, characteristic gesture of men who habitually chew *paan*.

"How frightening the heat is," the man said, as if speaking to himself.

She was not there the next day, or the day after that. Saeed looked for her every day, buying magazines he didn't need and fruit he couldn't afford as he waited for a glimpse of her. Often he missed the two o'clock bus in the hope she might come along for the two-thirty. Sometimes he missed that one too and had to take a rickshaw home. But she never came.

He grew restless and impatient at work. His mind wandered when he needed to concentrate; twice he sent in the incorrect grades to the principal for final exams. He frequently misquoted Ghalib and Iqbal, and one morning he forgot to take with him the test questions for Class 8.

At home he snapped at his wife and children.

"Is something wrong at school?" his wife asked while he was eating.

"Of course there's nothing wrong. Don't you see how hot it is? This kind of weather can drive a man out of his mind. And can't we have something else instead of *masur*? I'm sick of this *daal*." He pushed the tray away.

"But when I make *maash* you want *masur* and now you don't want . . ." she broke off, distraught. "Here, have some *lassi*, the yogurt is very sweet today."

He noticed how dough had caked around her finger nails and on the edges of her palms. Her fingers, thin and knotted, were ringless, he realized, and she wore no bangles. Gulping down the drink hastily, he handed the glass back to her.

That afternoon Saeed could not fall asleep. What he had thought of as madness before he now accepted as truth. He knew the woman in the black *burka* had become an obsession. But he also admitted now that no degree of rational thought or reasoning could compel him to deviate from that obsession.

His sleep at night was tormented by dreams in which he was always running, sometimes after a bus, and often after a dark nebulous cloud from which a pair of hands extended toward him as if to draw him in an embrace. In one dream, from which he woke up drenched in perspiration, he clasped in his arms a woman wrapped in a *burka* and as he fondled her body, the face masked by the veil, he realized that under the satiny *burka* she was naked.

During the day he pursued her in his thoughts, running after her until she turned to face him. But it was an anguished fantasy. He never saw her face clearly. The lineaments remained diaphanous, a hazy and obscure image, as if he were viewing it from a great distance. Every once in a while he also struggled with the poem he had been writing and found it to be a feeble, sterile struggle. He felt the gnawing change in himself, and his agony grew.

It was the last day of school. Saeed knew he would not be making this trip to the bus stop for a whole month unless he had to go in for a teacher's meeting, which was sometimes scheduled for the end of July, a week before school reopened. He had let the two-thirty bus go. Standing at the stop, fanning himself with a folded copy of the newspaper he had bought minutes ago, he let his eyes wander in all directions, searching for her. Not sure if he were imagining it or if it was indeed real, he inhaled a familiar scent, rose attar, the fragrance that had consumed him in his sleeping and waking hours. He spun to his right, then to his left. There were a dozen women at the bus stop. His mouth went dry as his gaze travelled frantically from hand to hand and feet to feet . . . she was there! He spotted and recognized the black sandals, he saw the hands, pale and lovely, the black bangles catching the light of the sun like flames leaping out in the darkness. When the bus arrived and people rushed toward it, he scurried forward in haste. I must not lose her today, he told himself over a violently pulsating echo of blood rushing to his head.

This time Saeed stayed close to her. Some women standing no more than a few inches from him grumbled that he was in the women's section, one tried to push him with her basket. The division was arbitrary, so he ignored their muttering and kept his eyes on her. Fifteen minutes later she got off at a stop he recognized as Shahalami and he got off with her.

She walked for nearly half a mile before turning into a residential area not unlike the one where he lived. The streets were dark and narrow, the houses lined up, one on top of another, huddled together, a little sky visible where the roofs ended. She turned into a gulley and Saeed followed her at a discreet distance; he didn't wish to frighten her. Some children played *gulee danda* and marbles on the cobbled street. He had not given any thought to what he was going to do. Would he talk to her, would he stop her and ask the way to some imaginary street, would he tell her who he was? A peddler with a clanking, narrow steel trunk strapped to the back of his bicycle and filled with stale pastries Saeed knew, trudged past him. "*Pashtry, pashtry,*" the man droned on interminably.

Without any warning, perhaps when he was momentarily distracted by the pastry-*wallah's* voice, she turned left into a gulley and was lost to view. He ran to the end of the gulley. There was no sign of her. She could have gone through one of the innumerable doors that lined the darkened alley on both sides. Which one? His heart beat with uncontrollable force. He gasped, cursing himself, cursing the peddler. He felt like an animal that had been trapped and was struggling to be free. "Oh God, oh God, help me," he whispered helplessly, hot tears streaming down his face.

⊷⟞◉⟝⊶

Razia had made lamb curry. Saeed could smell the aroma of meat cooked in spices, steamed with fresh sprigs of coriander. He heard her on the other side of the door, fiddling with the latch. When she opened the door he thrust a package into her hands.

"What's this," she asked. "Where's the fruit?" She followed him into their bedroom.

Silently he took the package from her hands and emptied it on the bed. A pair of shiny black sandals with thin leather straps, a set of black glass bangles spilling out of their white tissue paper wrapping with a musical jangle, and a tiny bottle.

Gingerly Razia picked up the bottle. "Attar of roses?" she said, looking at him incredulously.

A Peep-Hole Romance

The peep-hole was smaller than a keyhole but large enough for an eye to fit snugly against it. No one knew why or how it came to be in the center of a panel in the drawing-room door. The house was old, with a history of owners who fled, hurriedly, reluctantly, in great sorrow, to India at the time of Partition. Was it one of them who had painstakingly created this tiny opening? Or was it an accident, a carpenter's oversight? Perhaps it was the result of a child's game, an experiment with a new tool, or maybe there was a voyeur in the family who secretly drilled the hole, making it small enough as to go unnoticed. Then again, it may have been devised for the same purpose that the new occupants had endowed it with, an aperture through which the young, unmarried women in the family could take a first look at prospective bridegrooms.

Before Shama, her two aunts, Aunt A. and Aunt S., had come to this very hole to peer at the men who arrived to inspect and be inspected. For some reason, no one had taken the trouble to close up the hole even though the panels had been repaired at least twice, and several coats of paint had been applied to the door in the last twenty years. Little things like that didn't merit attention.

The opening was useful, because once you were in the drawing-room with the guests you could not make close observations without appearing audacious and impertinent. Special instructions to Nasiban, the fat, overly optimistic, animated matchmaker, made it possible for the gentleman in question to be seated on the sofa or the divan that faced the door with the hole. If by some mischance the arrangement of the guests proved unsatisfactory, Nasiban, who seemed rather adept at this sort of thing, cleverly moved people around during tea. Like her aunts, then, Shama was able to contemplate the scene minutely before going in.

The last man Shama had scrutinized through this secret opening had been a thick-set, balding doctor, the kind of man who never looks young and with whom one associates disagreeable things like belching, snoring, and swearing. Not romantic in the least. Later, when she was in the same room with him, Shama discovered he had a pleasant voice, a polite manner and intelligent eyes, but, unfortunately, that wasn't enough. She had judged too hastily, but what she saw now still failed to stir her, still didn't make her breathless with excitement.

This was the third bachelor to come with his mother and sisters to see Shama. Nasiban was quite upset when Aunt S. informed her Shama wasn't taken with him. She hinted in a politely cutting tone that if the young woman continued to be so fussy, she'd end up a spinster. Aunt S. tried to appease Nasiban and requested that she keep trying, please. Further, she told Shama she had no business flying so high in the clouds.

"You're not a fairy princess yourself, girl. Your nose isn't that small and fine either, and your complexion is just two shades away from what people might call dark. What do you want? A prince?"

"No, *Phupo*, not a prince, but then not someone who has a paunch to begin with and is nearly bald already. A few good years in the beginning at least, don't you think?"

"What nonsense! A man's a man. You have to see if he has education, a good job, if he can provide, and of course he shouldn't be a philanderer. You're not going to have Raj Kapoor or Dilip Kumar knocking at your door."

Shama and her aunt, both of whom thought going to films was as important as reading a new novel, rated Raj Kapoor and Dilip Kumar as the best-looking actors in Indian films, also the most romantic. However, Aunt S., who was married and had two young children, was not flying up in the clouds, whereas Shama, being only twenty-two, and overwhelmed by a sense of adventure, exhibited a certain tendency to be reckless, something her aunt constantly worried about. But Shama knew she could be bold. She had time.

As for the second gentleman, he didn't have a paunch, was quite lean, and his hair was long and straight and flat like the wings of a crow. His horn-rimmed glasses reminded Shama of a picture of Saadat Hasan Manto, the famous writer who drank himself to an early grave, but who in life had been known for his daring and outspoken fiction. This fellow, whose name was Shahid, made some attempts to cast sidelong glances at her while she was serving tea to his mother and younger sister, and later talked politics with Shama's mother and Aunt S. until Shama thought she would fall asleep right there in front of everyone.

What if he has no other passion in life except politics? she thought in horror. He seemed to have forgotten the purpose of his visit and was soon deeply engrossed in an exchange about Prime Minister Bhutto's shortcomings with Aunt S. and Shama's older brother, Mani. Well, that settled it. Everybody in her family were Bhutto loyalists. The fighting would never end.

The first visit was the one that Shama remembered clearly, every detail distinct and incandescent.

Pink, yellow and all shades of brown and beige had been discarded. She looked dark and sallow in all of them.

"Black will flatter your complexion, but unfortunately black is the color of mourning," Aunt S. expressed regret while scrutinizing the *shalwar-kameez* suits that had been spread out on Shama's bed. "I think this one would be best." She pointed to the *kameez* with a blue-and-red flowered print. "And the plain red silk *shalwar* along with your red chiffon *dupatta* will go well with it."

Since this was the first time Shama was to be seen, she was nervous and apprehensive. But Aunt S. was in control, and Shama didn't resist. Better her aunt than Amma, who just made her feel shy and who probably felt uncomfortable herself telling Shama to wear this or that, or informing her that her nose was too broad at the base and somewhat rounded, or that she was not fair enough to be truly marketable.

So the red and blue flowered print it was, a little powder, some rouge, a touch of red lipstick, and a warning not to talk too much as she always did.

"Men don't like chatty women," Aunt S. informed her in a matter-of-fact tone, "they prefer the demure, reticent type."

Shama giggled. Suddenly she felt impetuous. Why, she could be anything she wanted. She could be so shy and demure one would think there wasn't a tongue in her mouth, and she could also smile in that bashful, reticent way she had seen a hundred brides do in films. It would be easy, she knew.

Her aunt smiled with satisfaction. Both women stood in front of the mirror and viewed their handiwork. Yes, Shama looked pretty this evening; the red of the *dupatta* draped lightly over her shoulders was becoming, the little gold earrings swung playfully from her ear lobes, dancing with every movement of her head, catching the light and shimmering. After Aunt S. left the room to help Amma with the tea things, Shama closed the bedroom door and studied herself in the mirror a long time, from different angles, turning this way and that. She felt as if there were two of her, one observing the other with approval and awe. Patting the tiny curl on the side of her forehead, she smiled with satisfaction.

She liked him the moment she set eyes on him. Her breasts ached with a strange throbbing, a knot formed in her stomach. He was tall and his hair fell carelessly over a part of his wide forehead. His eyes had a brooding look and his clothes were clean and simple: pants, a white oxford shirt, full-sleeved, no tie, the collar open at the throat—oh so beautiful he was. Nasiban had provided them with the vital statistics ahead of time. He had just returned from England with a degree in mechanical engineering. He wants to go back to England, Nasiban had said, a bonus Aunt S. agreed readily, too readily, Shama thought.

But Shama didn't care where he took her as long as he took her. She wished he would talk to her, but after the first fifteen minutes of confused, agitated conversation in which Nasiban, her aunt, and the young man's mother participated and he mumbled a few words here and there, he just clammed up. During tea he seemed distracted and not once did he glance in her direction with any degree of interest. He doesn't like me, Shama thought mournfully, wondering whether it was her nose or her complexion that had failed her. Maybe her breasts, which were skimpy.

Nasiban returned apologetically several days later with what was meant to be a polite no. "The boy has an interest elsewhere, and the parents aren't agreeing," she explained, munching noisily on shortbread biscuits. "But listen to me, you don't worry at all. I have other matches in hand, better ones. A doctor, too." She lifted a finger and leaned forward conspiratorially.

Aunt S. and Amma had closed-door sessions with Abba and Shama's grandparents after which Aunt S. assured Shama that whatever happens is for the best, there is Allah's design in all things. But Shama was heartbroken, though she joked with her aunt.

"*Phupo*, who wants to go to England anyway, and who knows how many girlfriends he had while he was in England. Could you check, *huh?*"

But secretly she felt as if something precious had been wrenched from her. Slowly, the sense of loss gave way to anger. On Nasiban's next visit she came in while her aunt and her mother were conferring over tea and wafer biscuits in the drawing-room; bursting in on them, taking them by surprise, she told Nasiban she didn't want to see anyone else.

Unruffled, Nasiban just smiled complacently and continued to slurp tea from her cup. Aunt S. said, "Don't mind her. You know girls today, they're so stubborn."

A dry run followed during which Shama applied for and got a teaching position at the Model Girls School and it wasn't until the end of her third month there that Nasiban made another appearance. The balding doctor and the fellow obsessed with politics were Nasiban's next offerings. Finally, when Shama turned down both men, Nasiban grabbed her *burka* and stormed out of the house, avowing never to return.

Aunt S. evoked frightening images of spinsters.

"Do you remember my friend Amtulraza? The one who has a mustache and when she laughs her massive stomach jiggles? Her cousin wanted to marry her when she did her B.A. and she refused because he was too short and had tired, watery eyes. Now she wishes she hadn't turned him down. And Miss Razak? Your professor in Lahore College? Such stories about her, the poor woman, young boys trailing after her, singing obscene songs at her window?"

"*Phupo*, please," Shama pleaded, "none of this is helping. I'm not going to marry someone I don't feel *something* for, something at least!"

Her aunt looked at her sadly. For the first time Shama became aware of the silver streaks in Aunt S.'s hair, the deep lines that were carved along the sides of her mouth, the tiny folds of skin in threads around her eyes.

"*Phupo*, don't worry," she said reassuringly, "as you've said so many times, when it's God's will the right person will come along." Of course, God's will could bring the right *or* the wrong person to your door, and there could be no reversal of His will either.

And now she was peering through the hole again. But what was this? Facing the door was a young woman, no older than Shama herself and squirming uncomfortably in her seat, while Aunt S., Amma, and two other women, who might have been aunts or older sisters, were on the sofa at right angles to Shama's vision. And where was he? He was on the high-backed wooden chair right in front of her and at the level of her eye was the back of his head and his neck. Some preview this was going to be, Shama thought, her spirits dampened. This time a mutual family friend was the person responsible for this meeting. Nasiban wasn't there to perform her usual tricks with the seating arrangements. Shama missed the old crone.

Finally her gaze strayed to what was closest within the circle of her vision. Like a camera zooming in, she allowed her eye to travel over what she could see.

Hair, black, wavy, falling softly down to a tanned neck, a rumpled collar barely visible over the back of the chair, part of a broad shoulder. And then she saw a hand appear quietly to embrace the chair's rounded, carved arm. A broad-palmed hand, the fingers not too long, the nails clipped and clean, and silky hair covering the back of the hand like fine brush strokes on a canvas. She didn't know what she loved first: the hand, so still, yet so strong and expressive, or the nape of his neck where stray tendrils of his dark, curly hair spiraled like endless question marks. Her heart thrashed about in her chest with a force she couldn't control, the blood rushed to her face, making her feel warm.

She nearly ran to her room and locking the door behind her, stood in front of the long mirror on the armoire. Oh, she so wanted to be beautiful, desirable, so enchanting that when he saw her he would say, "This one is for me," just as she had said, running to her room, like a chant, "This one is for me." Her face was flushed. She quickly brushed off the beads of sweat that had gathered on her upper lip and her forehead. The image in the mirror was someone she didn't know, a woman whose eyes were luminous, whose hair was like a black cloud full of mystery, whose lips opened and closed like the rounded petals of a summer flower. And the outline of her breasts was clear, suggesting firmness, youth.

When Shama went to the drawing room later she didn't really talk to him. There just seemed no need for it, but he chatted with Mani, and she was happy to hear his voice; you can hear so much in a person's voice, especially when your own voice isn't in the way. He was a doctor and although Shama had decided she was going to stay away from men of science because they were so unromantic, she didn't care any more. It didn't matter, she realized, howling to herself in silent laughter at her foolishness.

Right away, without really looking into his eyes, and she couldn't look into his eyes from where she sat anyway, she knew he was saying, "This one is for me." She just knew.

During tea her glance wandered to the panel with the peep-hole. From afar it looked like a tiny speck, too small to be noticeable. She remembered suddenly how when they were children, she and her cousin Nadira had tried to close it up with chewing gum. First they just slapped the ball of gum, pink, wet, and gluey, onto the hole, attempting to flatten it against the wood, but the gum wouldn't stick and kept falling down. Finally, at her cousin's advice, they got a knitting needle and forced and shoved the gum into the hole until it was closed off. A knitting needle had come to the rescue again when the hole was cleaned out for Aunt A.'s preview sessions.

Once again Shama laughed to herself, as she had done so often that evening. She felt something at last.

⚫➡ New Beginnings ⬅⚫

Why the idea materialized, or what impelled it to gain momentum, Arifa didn't know. But one thing was certain; she couldn't shake it off, and this despite the fact that her day was filled with a clutter of tiring, laborious chores. A test on Iqbal's philosophy of the self had to be administered to her second period Urdu class, and another on Manto's short story "The New Law" had been given to a disgruntled sixth period class (the girls had wanted more time for preparation). Two sets of notebooks containing lengthy, muddled essays also waited to be marked, and there was the monthly staff meeting with Sister Magdalene (which, as always, dragged on endlessly and without resolution). And that was not all. After school, while other teachers returned home to leisurely hot lunches and long, undisturbed afternoon naps, and even the nuns retreated into the mysterious antechambers on the far side of the chapel, Arifa was in the school auditorium directing the annual Urdu play. This year it was Rahila Manzur's *The Demented School Teacher*.

For nearly eight years Arifa had directed the Urdu play willingly, without any qualms, even though there were three other Urdu teachers who could have done it. *Someone has to take the responsibility*, she kept telling herself, but it wasn't just from a sense of duty that she had directed the school play year after year. No, there was more. Every time she fashioned the play she felt a certain satisfaction that had little to do with a sense of accomplishment; there was an inner stirring she experienced, as if she were on the brink of some fresh and electrifying discovery. But something had changed this year. The play, along with its trappings, had become a burden. As a matter of fact, rehearsals, students' essays, and the long lectures—everything had begun to feel like millstones around her neck. Eventually she was compelled to rethink her dedication; not only that, but to her own surprise she found herself toying with the idea of early retirement.

"I would like to give the play to someone else this year," she announced to Sister Magdalene one afternoon during a free period.

The young nun gawked at her, rolled her blue eyes in exaggerated shock, as if Arifa had just announced, "Sister, the Pope has been shot!"

"But Mrs. Husain, you've always done the Urdu play!" Sister Magdalene exclaimed. Too attractive for a nun with her small, upturned nose and restless blue eyes edged with the thickest line of black lashes, Sister Magdalene had once been Jackie Brown, the daughter of an Anglo-Indian mother and an English father. When Arifa joined St. Mary's nearly ten years ago, Jackie was completing her Senior Cambridge and it was common knowledge that she was destined to be a nun. *What a waste*, Arifa had thought then. *What a waste*, Arifa said to herself now.

"Yes, but it is time for someone else to take charge. I don't have the energy I used to." Moved to a smile by Sister Magdalene's reaction, Arifa made an attempt at firmness. She had always admired the nuns for their purity of purpose and singlemindedness. Now here was something she could learn from these sisters of charity.

"You can't stop now," Sister Magdalene was saying, "you just can't, Mrs. Husain. Who will take over if you abandon the play?"

Take over? Abandon? What a sly one you are, Arifa thought affectionately. "Well, there's Noreen Ahmed and there's also Mr. Aziz. They could both do a fairly good job if they put some effort into it." However, Arifa had grave doubts that Noreen and Mr. Aziz, who was older than she was and complained constantly of a bad back, had either the expertise or the talent to direct effectively the annual Urdu play, or any other play for that matter. But she was not inclined to be critical this morning.

"I'm sure they'll do a reasonably good job," Sister Magdalene remarked petulantly, a pale, thin, profusely freckled arm extended toward Arifa. "But not as well as you." She paused, smiled, her small, rounded chin firmly set against the stiff white collar of her wimple. "You're a seasoned director, Mrs. Husain, you don't really mean you want to give up the play now, do you?"

Sister Magdalene was so young sometimes Arifa forgot she was the headmistress and a nun and addressed her as she would a former student. Arifa's husband had nicknamed her Maggie. He also thought she was too pretty to be cloistered at St. Mary's. It pleased Arifa when Sister Magdalene asked her for something only she could give, although she was careful not to concede too easily. She couldn't allow anyone, least of all this enchanting young thing whose pink face didn't seem to belong to the severe white habit that entombed it, to take advantage of her.

"Well Sister, it's too much work and I'm not so young any more. I cannot manage all by myself, really, I cannot."

"Tell you what, I'll ask Miss Ahmed to assist you, and Mr. Aziz can be asked for some help as well. Now promise you won't talk about quitting again." Sister Magdalene tipped her head to one side and smiled benevolently at Arifa.

Arifa sighed. True, she couldn't really relinquish the play. She shouldn't. It was the one thing that was all hers. She could do with it as she pleased, steer it in any direction she wished, interpreting it at will. The girls were pliant in her hands, they listened to her. And with the help she had been promised her burden might be easier to bear.

But Noreen Ahmed, who taught English and on occasion had expressed interest in drama, left to get married, remained absent for a whole week following Arifa's conversation with Sister Magdalene and therefore was no help at all. As for Mr. Aziz, he explained, in a small, apologetic voice which Arifa interpreted as a masculine whimper, that he tutored several students at his home after school and had absolutely no time, no time whatsoever. What other choice did Arifa have but to continue alone?

This afternoon rehearsal was like a load of bricks upon her back, her arthritis straddled her shoulders like a harness and the girls, perhaps sensing her distraction, were chatty and inattentive. *What do they talk about?* Arifa wondered irately. *Boys, what else.*

"Can we begin now?" She raised a hand grimly in query.

The girls fell silent and took their places on stage and off. Samina, playing the role of the psychiatrist, came on-stage with a lopsided grin mapped across her thin, shiny face. Her long hair swinging in a pony tail down her back, she made an awkward, hesitant entrance.

"Samina, does the script call for a smile?" Arifa asked dryly. "And remember you are a man. You must stop swaying your hips and thrashing your arms about. Stand upright, chest in . . . yes, your hand in your pocket, and pretend you have a pencil in the other hand."

Flattening a long, lean hand against her left thigh (since she didn't have a pocket), Samina twirled the imaginary pencil with the fingers of her right hand. Slim and angular, she stiffly advanced toward the girl who was playing the prostrate patient.

"And show some confidence," Arifa interjected, "you are a man, aren't you?"

This was the moment, if Arifa wanted to pinpoint it, when the idea that had jiggled in her head like a loose spring in a ballpoint pen, suddenly surfaced with clarity. She found it impossible to push it aside and focus on what the girls were doing on stage. Again and again, like a beggar's persistent hand, the thought tugged for attention.

She could think of no other way. Time was forging ahead with speed. She must broach the subject with her husband without delay. Arifa was not a person who waited to do things. Always impetuous, though not reckless, she disliked lingering over decisions, procrastinating. A glance at her watch confirmed she had another hour of rehearsal. *If the girls cooperate, an hour will pass quickly*, she hastened to assure herself.

"Yes, that's better Samina. Now Jabin, you come in from the right just as Samina starts a conversation with the patient. You are the orderly, so act like one. You have seen enough of them, have you not?"

Arifa sat down on a chair close to the stage. Something was wrong. Her words, huddling upon one another, seemed to be getting caught in her throat, and the sound of the girls' voices was vibrating in her ears like the flapping of a *dupatta* in a sudden gust of wind. With her hand on her neck, she swallowed the ball of spit that was lodged in her throat like a cotton swab.

The idea was quite simple. Too simple, really. What she had in mind was a straightforward adoption, not one of those complicated legal situations lumbering along under the weight of this technicality and that. No, this would be a transaction of love. Arifa was pleased with the way she turned the phrase. And surely Mustafa would have no objection. It wasn't as if he were an infant who had to be taken in and raised to manhood. He was twenty-five, married and already a father himself. All that was done. *So little left to do except call him her son.*

The more she pondered the idea, the more tenaciously it fastened itself upon her heart. Mustafa would become *their* son, hers and Naseer's. He was Naseer's older sister's boy, and as a nephew he had been attentive and caring. As a son he would be more. Of course he wouldn't be answerable for their every need, but he would be here, close by and available, just as her Raza might have been had he been living in Pakistan.

Excitement welled up in her like bubbles rising on the surface of milk coming to a boil. The script fell from her hands, slipping noise-lessly to the auditorium floor. Mustafa will rush to her with his assent, she thought as she bent to retrieve the fallen script.

She remembered clearly, as though it were only yesterday, how Mustafa and Raza played together all afternoon in the lawn in their bungalow in Gulberg. How close the two boys had been as children. Arifa brooded with sadness over the distance that developed between them when Raza went to America. But men are like that, she told her-self, unable to sustain relationships across great distances.

"Mrs. Husain, should I come in from the left or the right?" It was Jabin. She was standing uncertainly in the center of the stage, alone at that moment, nervously fidgeting with the front edges of her white cot-ton shirt.

"From the right, girl. Did we not establish that the entrance to the office is from the right? Everyone should be coming in from there, understand?" Despite her resolve to sound firm, her voice cracked and her tone faltered.

The girls tittered in response to her admonition. Arifa shook her head in dismay while Jabin stared down at the floor, pouting; cast as the orderly in the play, she felt dissatisfied with her role.

"Start again, Jabin, and be sure to keep fussing with the duster on your shoulder." Why was it so difficult for them to act?

"Yes, Mrs. Husain," Jabin muttered glumly, reaching with her hand for the rolled up *dupatta* that doubled as duster this afternoon.

Why, it was not that Mustafa reminded her of Raza. No, that would be a silly reason to adopt Mustafa, quite silly. And they were so differ-ent. Even as children one had been a clown, while the other took every-thing so seriously, a little like his uncle. Often Raza climbed over Mustafa, tickling him in the ribs just to see him become helpless with laughter and gasping, begging Raza to stop. There was no physical resemblance either. Raza was taller, wore glasses, and his hair was already thinning like his father's, while Mustafa was not nearly as tall and his hair was thick and wavy.

That she was extremely fond of Mustafa had much to do with it, she knew. Yes, of course that was it, and it wasn't difficult to be fond of him. Last November when she was sick with a stubborn flu bug and had to stay home from work for a whole week, he and his young wife Shakira, came to see her regularly and they never came empty-handed. He always had for her a box of *burfi*, *gulab jamun*, or carrot *halwa*, her favorite. And was there ever a frown on his face when she or Naseer asked him for a favor, like getting the car serviced or fixing the TV antenna when it went haywire after that terrible dust storm in June? What more could she ask for in a son?

The patient was sprawled out on the floor in what was meant to be a fit of dementia, but all Rohi, the patient, could muster was a feeble writhing of her arms and legs. Samina, who should have been bent over her solicitously as the orderly wrestled her down, was standing nearby chortling. Jabin, meanwhile, her hand dutifully clasping and unclasping the duster as instructed, leant over Rohi, her face contorted with amusement. Arifa sighed. *Drama this is not, this is a spoof.* The girls were obviously as distracted as she.

"We will stop now," Arifa said. "Rehearsal same time tomorrow, and I'm warning you girls, this giddiness will not do at all. You need to get serious, there is not much time left." *No, not much time left at all.*

"Yes, Mrs. Husain." Her students bounded from the stage like little children scurrying off to begin a game of hide-and-seek. To think that in another three or four years some of them would be married and in another year become mothers. Why, so little time was left, Arifa mused as she left the school auditorium, her students following behind whispering, excited, suddenly imbued with energy.

"*Salaamalekum*, Mrs. Husain," they chirped in chorus before veering off in the direction of the school tuckshop where they would eat spicy *samosas* doused with thick, tart tamarind chutney.

The November afternoon was still. No breeze, no stirring of fallen leaves, no sound of children's voices. The sun touched Arifa sharply, its shimmering glare overwhelming her. Shielding her eyes with her hand, she made her way to the veranda to wait for Naseer. Autumn had begun to sere the trees. Brown, decaying leaves lay in sodden heaps around the umber tree trunks. It wouldn't be long before one forgot that these very leaves had once, in emerald brilliance, graced the naked, spindly branches that now reached upward feebly toward a cloudless sky.

What was it, what had Raza written about Massachusetts? The season had another name there. Fall. Although Arifa had tried her best to shake off the association, again and again the word dredged recollections of Raza's disastrous fall from an old oak in their backyard when he was eight. That was when Naseer worked for the police and they lived in Gulberg in a sprawling government bungalow.

Watching from the kitchen window when Raza and Mustafa climbed the tree, she had thought, *I must tell them to be careful.* But the rapidly browning onions for *bhagar* in the frying pan caught her attention, and her mind turned away from the boys. Raza's scream a few minutes later made her race out of the kitchen in panic, the ladle with which she had been stirring the onions held aloft in her hand like a sword.

"Why weren't you more careful?" she addressed Mustafa roughly while she cradled her son's head in her lap. "Go get the driver, tell him to hurry with the car."

Later, as the car taking them to the hospital turned on the driveway, she caught a glimpse of Mustafa from the car window. She had forgotten all about him. He stood still, dwarfed by the tall columns on the veranda, his face drained of color, and she remembered the harsh tone she had used with him. How could she have been so inconsiderate?

"Fall begins slowly," Raza had written in his last letter to her, "so you don't really know what's happening. Gradually there are shades of orange and red everywhere and you put it all together with flowers, forgetting it's the death of a season. Nobody calls it autumn here, it's fall, a wonderful time of the year, but it's short-lived. I wish you could see it, you would love the brilliant colors."

Yes, she would, she would like to see the color he wrote about. But how curious that autumn should be a carnival of color and that in her son's mind all previously grounded images of what bare trees, dark discolorations among vegetation, and the redolence of decaying leaves imply had been relinquished, replaced. She looked around her. She couldn't see what was not there. Like her young students, she was unable to pretend this afternoon.

Naseer wouldn't show up for another twenty minutes. Well, that would give her time to think further. She made herself comfortable on the bench on the veranda from where she could easily spot her husband when he drove into the school compound. The girls from her play were nowhere in sight. Except for Sister Bertha, who stayed behind to police the veranda while all the other nuns went in for lunch, and the dark, wiry sweeper who sleepily thrashed his straw *jharu* about at one end of the veranda raising thin clouds of dust, no one was around.

"Good afternoon, Sister." How ridiculous that poor Sister Bertha had to be left out to patrol the school veranda. Barely able to walk, she was also so mild-mannered and gentle that if she was compelled to raise her voice in an outcry she would not be able to make herself heard. The middle-aged nun, rotund and bent, lumbered past Arifa, smilingly nodding a response to her greeting.

Arifa noticed that the afternoon sun had saturated the atmosphere with crystalline brightness. In her mind, too, some of the earlier ambiguities that had muddled her thinking slowly began to clear up. She felt certain that Mustafa would be touched by her proposal. Her head resting against the dusty back of the bench, she closed her eyes and luxuriated in the warmth the thought had generated, her earlier feelings of physical discomfort and the pain in her neck now dissipated.

She began making plans for a party. All the relatives, a few close friends, Mr. Aziz and Mrs. Ahmed from St. Mary's, certainly Maggie. If only her niece Zenab were here. She would approve. Arifa would not have to explain herself to Zenab, yes, Zenab, earnest and loyal, would understand why she must adopt Mustafa. *What a pity Zenab too is in America. What is happening? What is this call that has taken children away from their homes, made them careless, forgetful?*

Lost in reverie, Arifa failed to notice Naseer drive up. He honked, startling her.

In the car she didn't bring up the subject of adoption right away. For one thing Naseer was already giving her the details of the letter from Raza that must have come by the morning mail, and he didn't like to be interrupted when he was talking. *It's something that comes with being a civil servant for so long,* Arifa thought. Also, she didn't have the right words as yet with which to preface her suggestion. So she let her husband talk.

Now retired, Naseer spent the better part of his mornings and afternoons alone at home. He left the house only for his early morning walk and later to pick up Arifa from school. After breakfast he pored intently over the *Pakistan Times*, then sat in his favorite armchair close to the window looking out on the street and opened a book on history. Later, he listened to very old Indian film songs on his tape recorder. This last preoccupation surprised Arifa because in all these years he had never expressed any interest in music. Now, quite suddenly, a year into his retirement, he had begun listening with earnest diligence to songs from the twenties and thirties. Kanan Devi, Zohra Bai Ambalewali, Sehgal and Begum Akhtar raised doleful voices out of their bedroom, snapping the brittle silence of their house.

Naseer drove his car himself since he didn't trust anyone else with it, except Raza of course, who was not in Pakistan now. Although they could easily afford a part-time chauffeur, Naseer made it clear he didn't want one. "I enjoy driving," he insisted while he was recuperating from a gall bladder operation, and Arifa pressed him to hire a driver. City traffic was a young man's adventure and she feared he would over-tax himself. But he was adamant, so she let the matter rest.

"Raza is moving to a bigger house. He writes they have a guest bedroom now ready and he and Batul are waiting for us." Naseer spoke with confidence, as though he had already been to the new house in Massachusetts, seen the spare bedroom firsthand. "He says the area they're moving to is really nice."

Why shouldn't it be nice? But does it really matter? Raza can go anywhere, even as far as a thousand miles, and the distance between us will not be diminished. Why must he be so far away? If I wake up in the middle of the night with a sharp piercing pain in my chest and know I am going to die, will he be there to clasp my hand? And when I close my eyes in death, will his face be the last image I carry to the grave? The questions gnawed at her, making her restive. Sighing, she closed her eyes and thought about Mustafa again.

"I think we should adopt Mustafa." The words slipped out of her mouth before she could arrange them to satisfaction. She turned nervously to Naseer.

His gaze was pinned on the road ahead. But she saw his shoulders twitch. *He's laughing to himself. What will he say?* Arifa wondered. She waited like a child, who, surprised by her own boldness in the presence of an elder, waits bravely and helplessly for reprimand.

He remained silent. She examined his profile closely, noting as if for the first time, that the sharpness of his aquiline nose and the firm set of his lips increased the sternness of his expression. So often she wondered how he would react if their roof fell on them or there was an earthquake and they had to run, the image of a panicked, out-of-control Naseer failed to take hold in her mind.

"You're not serious, I hope," he finally said, his question followed by a grunt that Arifa recognized as a snicker.

"I'm quite serious, and you had better stop laughing. I do not mean a legal adoption of course, I'm not stupid. I mean a symbolic adoption, a sort of transaction of . . . of love." In telling the phrases sounded sappy and feeble. She decided to make a new start. "Mustafa will know we want him to be more than your nephew, you know, more like our son. What do you think?"

"I think you are out of your mind, Arifa. Maggie badger you about the play again?"

"No, no, Maggie has nothing to do with this. Please be serious for a moment. It will be like having two sons, one in America and one right here with us, within driving distance. He's such a fine young man, and I'm so fond of him, and we all get along so well." Arifa felt emotion rise in her throat like a sob. Placing a hand on her mouth, she coughed awkwardly.

"I'm not denying any of this," Naseer said impatiently, "but we see him regularly, and he's there when we need him, and so is his wife. So what's this nonsense about adopting him? You're just overworked. I think you should talk to Maggie about some help with the play."

"I did, and that's not it at all. I'm not depressed, not more than usual that is. I've given the matter a great deal of thought, I didn't just come up with the idea out of the blue, you know." She turned her gaze away from Naseer's hand on the steering wheel, a calm hand, the long, bony fingers relaxed, self-assured.

"Hmm," was all she got out of him.

Arifa told herself to put the discussion off until they were home. *He's not one to talk much while driving, and this isn't a chit chat, this is serious business.*

At a red light on Ferozepur Road Arifa rolled down the car window a few inches for some air. Looking out, she questioned as she had a hundred times before, how anyone, anyone at all, could maintain sanity while driving through this pandemonic, chaotic traffic. Milling about were cars, Toyotas mostly and Suzukis, along with old buses lopsided from the weight of their passengers, clamorous rickshaws, tongas pulled by spindle-shanked, skinny horses frothing at the mouth, also mangy dogs with lolling tongues, and tireless pedestrians who valiantly wound their way in an out of this obstreperous maze with the craftiness of master chess players. Just as she had made up her mind to close her eyes and lean back in her seat for a few moments of rest, a motorcycle suddenly screeched to a halt almost at arms' length from her face.

Its passengers clung to each other with a ferocity that startled Arifa. Sandwiched between the mother, who was wearing a black *burka*, and the father, who couldn't have been much older than Mustafa, sat a child, three perhaps, or maybe four. With his arms he clasped his father's waist, while the mother's arms girdled both father and son from either side. Absently Arifa wondered how safe it was for the three of them to be hitched on the motorbike in this fashion. The light turned green and the three zoomed ahead, the young man's white *shalwar* flapping noisily, the child pressing closer to his father's broad back, his grip around his waist tightening. The woman bent over them both guardedly.

At the door Mustafa greeted Arifa and his uncle with his usual cheerful, loud *salaamalekum.*

"Come in, come in, what a pleasant surprise," he said, opening the door wide for them.

Arifa realized they should have called. She and Naseer always made their visits on Friday and she always called first. Today was only Monday.

Draped around Mustafa's legs was his three year old son. Arifa hadn't forgotten to bring him a bag of toffees.

"Here, son, it's what you've been waiting for," she said, dangling the bag in front of his face, waiting for him to come to her. He stared at her cautiously, then longingly at the bag in her hand, and finally extended a tiny plump arm toward her without letting go of his father's leg. She tweaked his cheek and relinquished the small plastic bag.

"Say *salaam* to Dadima," Mustafa admonished. The boy responded by shrinking further behind his father's person. "He just woke up from his nap," Mustafa explained apologetically.

"Yes, yes, let him be," Arifa said with a smile. "Where's Shakira?"

"In the kitchen finishing up the dishes, I'll get her."

Again Arifa stretched her hands toward Mustafa's son who had unwrapped a toffee by now and was trying unsuccessfully to bite into it. "Come here and give Dadima a hug."

He grinned this time, the toffee now lodged whole in his mouth, shook his head and hid behind a chair. She looked up to find Naseer watching her with amusement.

"He's just playing hard to get," Naseer offered comfortingly. "Bring him two bags next time."

Mustafa returned with Shakira. She looked pretty this evening, her face flushed, perhaps due to the heat in the kitchen. Arifa rose from the sofa to embrace her, catching as she held the young woman close for a minute, a whiff of raw onions, garlic, perspiration and perfume, all mixed together, a housewife's odor, pungent, familiar.

The two women fell into conversation quickly. Shakira was intelligent, not keenly so, but she had a perception of things that sometimes surprised and pleased Arifa. Not too long ago she made a remark about women being left alone in the house too much and ignored when they went out, except by oglers. Arifa hadn't known Shakira to ponder over such matters before. She agreed and encouraged the young woman to continue her education and go on to a masters as soon as the baby was old enough for nursery school.

For a while Shakira and Arifa joined their husbands in a discussion of Prime Minister Nawaz Sharif's new economic program and Benazir Bhutto's discomfiting alliance with him.

"Well, so much for integrity," Naseer remarked sardonically.

"What do you mean?" Arifa spoke up angrily. "Did she have a choice? It was that or jail sooner or later on some false pretext, or exile, or who knows what else."

"Yes Uncle, she's playing by their rules, it's true, but at least she's still playing," Shakira said bravely, knowing how much Naseer disliked Benazir.

"The important thing is they're not fighting any more, we have some peace finally," Mustafa interjected hastily.

Shakira took the hint. "Auntie, have you seen the new silk suits at the Shadman market? It's Indian silk, lovely and not too expensive either."

Shakira was in her early twenties and reminded Arifa of her students. As she talked her dark eyes widened repeatedly like a child's, and she had a habit of giggling with every sentence that came out of her mouth. She had a pleasant face, not beautiful, but charming, the skin clear and unmarred. There was a brightness about her. *Is it youth?*

"Blue suits you, Shakira," Arifa said, fingering the younger woman's sleeve.

"Really, Auntie? You don't think it makes me look dark?"

"Of course not, I think it looks very good on you."

"You like everything I wear," Shakira reacted with her quick characteristic laugh. "I'll get tea now."

Arifa glanced at Mustafa, who was listening intently to something Naseer was saying. His head was bent to one side, his gaze riveted to some point on his uncle's person, his face clothed in an expression of seriousness. *My son Mustafa*, Arifa rolled the words over on her tongue silently, letting the phrase linger in her head, *My son.*

While she watched the men, Mustafa's son, who had earlier disappeared with his mother into the kitchen, suddenly reappeared, his face grubby from a combination of saliva and sugary, gummy brown toffee, and going up to his father, wrapped himself around his legs again. Absently, without taking his eyes off his uncle's face, Mustafa stroked his son's hair with his right hand. The boy rubbed his face on his father's white *shalwar*. He resembles his mother, Arifa thought, his eyes wide like almonds, his hair brown and curly, and with her lips, small, tight and sharply outlined.

What will my grandchild look like? Arifa had never really given much thought to the question before and she was disturbed that a definite picture didn't take shape in her mind. She knew she didn't want the baby to have Naseer's nose, and she would like a boy. But all she succeeded in conjuring up at this moment was smallness, little else. Upset, she irately shrugged the thought away.

Her attention shifted to the new cushion covers on the armchairs. They were a bright, eye-catching yellow with turquoise and red birds in flight among a profusion of multicolored flowers. The satin stitching was well-ordered, all edges flawlessly tidy. On the table before her was a matching yellow tablecloth with the same motif. Shakira had been hard at work it seemed. Arifa was pleased that the room carried an air of neatness, that there were no gossamer cobwebs dangling from the corners between the ceilings and the walls, no fine layer of dust on the wooden arms of the chair on which she was seated. How fortunate they had been to find someone like Shakira for Mustafa. *A good daughter-in-law is the last link to a son's heart.*

Arifa beckoned the child to her again. "Come here, come to Dadima," she called, her arms stretching toward the boy. "Come to me."

He's such a precious little thing, but why does he hold on to his father so tenaciously? It isn't healthy for a child to be so possessive, and he's made such a mess with Mustafa's shalwar, *streaking it with dark brown smudges.*

"Come on now," she reiterated. The child continued to squirm and giggle beneath his father's legs, protesting frequently.

"Go," Mustafa pushed the boy away from him, toward Arifa. "Go, you silly boy, she only wants to give you a kiss." Mustafa coaxed him and the child became stiff like an autumn branch. Then, leaving the sofa, Mustafa lifted his son in his arms and carried him over to Arifa.

The boy's face fell, his eyes moistened.

"It's all right," Arifa said awkwardly, patting the child's small dark curls, "he's probably scared of me." She laughed, noticing just then, as Shakira came in with tea, a questioning look in Naseer's eyes.

For some crazy reason, the school play broke into her thoughts.

⊷═◉◉═⊶

"Well?"

"Well what?"

"Why didn't you say anything to Mustafa?"

"Do you really want to know or are you making fun of me again?"

"I'm not making fun of you, Arifa, I really want to know."

Retirement has mellowed him, Arifa thought. "I've changed my mind."

"Oh?"

"Yes."

"Why?"

"The boy, Mustafa's son, I don't feel . . . I don't feel what I should for him."

Naseer turned to look at her, something he rarely did while driving. It was too dark in the car to see the expression on his face, but Arifa knew she had caught him by surprise with her remark.

She continued. "He's an adorable child and very dear, but that's all. I don't feel the same surge of affection for him that I feel for his father."

"But you were planning to adopt Mustafa, not his whole family."

Why was it he always saw just so much, missing the rest, as if there were a curtain shielding it? "It has to be the whole family, don't you understand? How can I adopt Mustafa when I have this . . . this deficit. If Mustafa is to be our son, his children are to be our grandchildren, I mean they will be anyway, but . . ." She broke off helplessly.

Arifa was perplexed by her husband's silence. Perhaps he was condemning her for being so callous. Or perhaps he knew her better than she thought he did. Perhaps he too didn't feel the same surge of affection for the child as he did for the child's father. *But that is not right. That's not how it should be. Something is wrong. With her. Has the spring dried up inside her? Is she too old and tired to feel maternal passion? Is she asking for more than she can give? More than she should have? Has selfishness crept into her heart, tightening its sinews, making it less vulnerable?*

Leaning back in her seat she closed her eyes and wondered what her son might be doing this very moment. It was past ten, which meant it was early morning in Massachusetts. He would be getting ready to go to the hospital. Batul would be up too, drowsy-eyed and slow, making breakfast and he would ask for another cup of tea while his first one sat half-finished before him, cold. Perhaps he had given up on tea and now drank coffee, black and bitter, such an unhealthy brew. Maybe he was sitting next to a window with white shutters, the kind she had seen in the photographs he sent home, and gazing at the fall colors, thinking,

"Amma will love this." Or maybe he was already at the hospital, bent over a patient whose heart was giving out and who needed his ministrations.

While darkness overtook them like a stealthy prey-stalker, Arifa felt her own heart flutter as if it were a weightless object let loose in the confines of her chest. She glanced at her husband, unable to see his face except when the lights from an oncoming car illuminated it. Her thoughts returned to her students. The young girls whose laughter was so unfettered and who didn't know how to act. *But they're eager. And they're pliant. They are mine to teach, to instruct.* They were hers.

The Notebook

Quickly Salma ran to the door as he rattled the latch. He didn't like standing in the gulley outside his house, waiting as if he were a guest.

"People in the street start wondering where your wife is, what she's doing when you've been knocking and there's no sign of her," he shouted when he was inside the door. "This is the third time that you've made me wait." She avoided his gaze. "Why do you take so long?" he barked as she turned to walk away from him toward the kitchen.

"I was in the kitchen," she mumbled, adjusting the lock of hair that had escaped from her braid, "making *roti*." She didn't stop because the stove was cold and should he decide to come into the kitchen before going into the bathroom to splash water over his face and change from his pants and shirt into *shalwar* and *kameez*, he'd certainly know she had lied, and then he might hit her. Turning the switch on the stove, she fumbled with the matchbox for a few seconds before taking out a match. Her fingers trembled when she struck the match-head and held it to the gas. The stove came to life with a muffled boom.

The thin, blackened pan was already in place, and when it began to heat up she took out a handful of dough and swiftly rolled it into a round ball. She worked feverishly, still apprehensive that he might walk in and find her rolling the dough and no *roti* in sight.

Salma couldn't remember exactly when she had started lying to her husband. Perhaps it all began when he brought her a new notebook which had shiny covers, the front adorned with a picture of red and yellow flowers against a green background, on the back a picture of green birds flying among tangled branches and a few words underneath: "The reason birds can fly and we can't is simply that they have perfect faith, for to have faith is to have wings." A certain Sir James Barrie was the author of this touching thought. Inside, the pages were bluish-white and lined.

Salma's husband wanted her to start putting the daily accounts in it.

51

"Begin today and put down everything you give the washerman, the *sabziwallah*, anything else you get, like *massalas* or fruit. Don't leave out even a paisa. You are spending too much and not keeping an eye on anything." He handed her the notebook and a set of yellow lead pencils as if she were a student getting ready for an important exam.

The first week Salma diligently set everything down, even the fifty paisas she spent on red dye for her old cotton *dupatta* that needed a little brightening. He checked the accounts regularly like a rigorous schoolmaster, occasionally making corrections where she had made addition mistakes. Salma watched him while he ran the tip of the pencil down the figures in the column, pausing every now and then, wrinkling his brow so that the expression on his face turned into a scowl, then continuing, sometimes mumbling addition under his breath, a hissing sound that reminded Salma of the way he muttered verses over the beads of his *tasbih* after prayers. She held her breath and waited while he examined her work, still not used to the sudden reprimands he dealt her when he detected an error.

One morning, just after she had finished putting in the column two rupees, fifty paisas for the vegetables she had bought from the vendor outside her front door, placing with care the amount under one rupee seventy-five paisas for turmeric and cumin, she didn't shut and put away the notebook as usual. In the kitchen the *daal* was slowly simmering on the stove. The air was thick with the sharp, spicy aroma of *maash*, so different from the other lentils. She had already washed the baby eggplants and cut them into thin, even strips. When she threw the glistening purple peels into the trash can, she felt a twinge of sadness; the color was so luxurious, the gleam so brilliant, like swatches from a royal robe, and what a shame they must be thrown, discarded. One day last week, when she was shelling peas, the tiny, perfectly rounded, firm green peas had seemed to her like emerald beads and she had thought she might dry them to string into a necklace.

It was only ten-thirty; her husband wouldn't be home until one and the *daal* could simmer a while longer. Feeling lazy, she stretched her legs on the bed and, the notebook open in her lap, she stared out the window next to her bed. There wasn't much to see, just some shiftless black crows on a neighbor's low wall, beyond that a pallid sky with small, insipid clouds that gave promise of neither rain nor shade. Absently caressing the yellow lead pencil with her fingers, Salma closed her eyes. Then, sitting up, she wrote her name down on the page where she had just finished putting the day's accounts. First she penned her name the way she would if she were doing it in a hurry, signing a form perhaps, or an identity card. 'Salma', she wrote again, this time slowly, with a flourish, the rims of the *seen* prominent and distinct, the length of the *lam* tall and elegant, the *meem* curved like a nascent spring tendril, and finally the *yey* orbed, a new moon. But she didn't stop after that, she didn't slide the notebook under her pillow as was her custom. She stared at her name. Like the sudden flash of lightening on a dark, silent night, a couplet from a famous poem jumped into her head.

It is a heart, not a stone or a brick,
Why then should it not well up with pain?

Turning to a new page, fresh, white and unsullied, Salma began writing the couplet. With the last word in, she sketched, above and below the lines, a small flower, just three or four tiny petals, and then added a leaf, a design to embellish what she had written. That was when she remembered her collection.

She had written on a *takhti* with reed pens and black ink when she was a child, the words on the greenish-yellow clay wash under her hand as she dragged the pen's nib thick with viscous ink coming to life as if there was some magic she had wielded. Graduating to holder pens and paper later when she was older, she always spent her last paisa on buying new nibs for transcription. But she wrote little after she passed tenth class, except letters to her friend Shahida who had moved to Dubai with her husband soon after their marriage. There was a flurry of correspondence between the two women in the beginning, but then the cost of the airmail envelopes became unmanageable. Also, Shahida had less and less to say, so the letters ceased. But the writing didn't end altogether. Occasionally Salma copied verses from poems in magazines she bought when she had a few rupees left over from the month's allowance her father entrusted to her care for household rations. Using pages torn out of her younger sister's school notebook, she wrote neatly and with care, without wasting space. At night, when her parents had gone to sleep and her sister was curled up under her blanket next to her, she recited or hummed the verses to herself.

The carefully folded papers containing her treasure of poems and couplets still lay between the red brocade *kameez* she wore on the day of her wedding and the pomegranate-red *dupatta* with the wide gilt edging and long golden strands that fell on her face like a shimmering shower when she was a bride. She had never looked at the poems in all the time she had been married. And when a year passed, she forgot she had them in the steel trunk that had come with her dowry, snug between the folds of her bridal clothes.

But now the new notebook was in her hands, and she remembered.

First she tore out the accounts, neatly, so the binding on the inside did not appear disfigured. She didn't want to keep anything, not even a jagged edge, no matter how tiny, to remind her of what had once been in this notebook. Then, forgetting the *daal* cooking on the stove with a steady sibilant sound, she painstakingly transferred to the notebook every word from those crushed and faded pages which still exuded a fragrance of the turmeric and rose attar mixture which she had vigorously rubbed into her skin on the eve of her wedding. Some of the gold spangles from her *dupatta* had fallen into the creases in the papers, making them glitter. She blew them away.

Twice she had to sharpen the pencil with the used blade her husband had given her for this purpose. Once, in her eagerness to finish a couplet before running to the kitchen to stir the ladle in the pot, she cut herself, just a nick, below the nail. A droplet of blood jumped up and sat still, like a ruby, on the tip of her finger.

So when her husband asked, "Are you taking good care of the notebook?" she smiled and said, a little audaciously, "Yes. I'm putting every paisa down."

Looking satisfied, he unrolled the prayer mat and stood for the afternoon prayer. "*Allaho Akbar, Allaho Akbar*," he recited, his hands raised to his ears. In Salma's ears his murmuring faded as she went away to heat his food. Her heart pounded. She had lied. What if he asked to see the notebook? But he was hungry and tired and as soon as he finished his food, he stretched out on his bed, turned on his side, his arm following the contour of his stocky body, the thick-knotted, fleshy fingers spread out on his thigh, just where his shirt ended and his *dhoti* began. Within minutes he was snoring.

Since there were no magazines to copy more verses and poems from, Salma became restless. One afternoon, while her husband slept with his back to her, she closed her eyes and started making up a verse, just like that, cursorily, not something elaborate, just a simple line at first and then another to complete the couplet. Excitement made her jittery. Her palms became sweaty and her breath came fast. She slipped off her *charpai*, taking care she didn't make any noise that might wake her husband, and went to the antechamber where the trunk was stored with other suitcases and bags. There she retrieved the notebook from under the red brocade shirt and quickly, her fingers trembling with apprehension and exhilaration, she hastily wrote down the rhyme she had created in her head, not caring anymore if the script was fancy or not.

> Of the restless heart, of the night of waiting,
> Let us speak, you and I.
> Let your heart be unafraid, let dread not restrain,
> Of spring let us speak, you and I.

In another week she had another verse. Usually when she was washing her hair in the morning after her husband had left for work, or when she was leaning against the front door, waiting for the *sabziwallah* so she could get potatoes, fresh hot chilies, crisp green-leafed coriander, and whatever vegetables looked worth the price he asked that day, the words dropped into her head. Strung together in rhythms, they left her trembling and fearful, for she did not understand where they came from, or why. There was a time, when, just as her husband pulled her shirt up and threw himself on her, she closed her eyes and two couplets flitted in, glided around her, as if they were garlands of cambeli, of red roses.

> That place of light, the starry heavens,
> Of that world let us speak, you and I.
> No tears then, no word of woe on our lips,
> Of friendship let us speak, you and I.

In two more weeks there was a full *ghazal*. Having completely ignored the accounts, she was taken by surprise when her husband asked, "So, you must have filled half the notebook now? Show me, I want to see how this month was."

"The accounts?" she stuttered, her heart hammering against her ribs in fierce rhythms. Her stomach cramped.

"Yes, where is the notebook?" He had finished eating and was lying down in readiness for his afternoon nap. Running a thick, broad palm over his bristly mustache, he said, this time loudly. "What, are you deaf now? Where is the notebook? Show it to me."

Salma said, her voice weak as if it had sunk into a well, "I'll get it. It's in the other room."

When she stood on the veranda she tried to think of an excuse. But instead, one word, then a phrase, then a line, then two, a couplet, crowded her thoughts so that she had no control over this deluge that filled her head like a river in flood.

> I had longed for glowing radiance,
> For a ray of light in darkness.
> I had tried to conquer the storm,
> To seek a shore beyond every wave.

"It's lost," she was saying. Standing by her husband's *charpai*, her head buzzing, feeling hot all over her body as if in the grip of a fever, she said, "It's lost. It's been lost for a long time. I didn't tell you because I thought you might get upset."

He raised himself on his elbows and glared at her. Salma saw his face cloud with anger, become dark. He sat up. His hand flew in the air as if it were not attached to his body. "Lost? You can't even take care of a notebook, you stupid woman!"

"Have you never lost anything? It was only a notebook," she heard herself say, the words ringing in her ears as if someone else had uttered them.

"Only a notebook? Did your father pay for it?" He swung his legs over the side of the *charpai* and, looming over her, slapped her. "What have you done with it? Have you been writing letters to your lover?"

"How can you say this to me, your own wife?" She felt moisture fill her eyes, felt it searing down her cheeks, but there was no accompanying sob and her voice didn't crack.

"You are so clever all of a sudden, so quick with an answer, I see. What have you been up to? Huh?" And he slapped her again so she fell against the side of the *charpai*, hitting her head on its wooden leg. "Get out of my sight."

She was surprised she didn't feel any pain. There was warm, red blood on her hand where she touched her forehead with it. Slowly she got up and went out to the veranda.

> I had longed to find love in a stony heart,
> See a glimmer of light in dying eyes.

She rinsed her face with cold water from the tap in the bathroom, then tore a strip from the edge of her *dupatta* and tied it around her head, covering the wound, which was still bleeding.

It wasn't his fault. He had been a good husband, he had held her in an embrace so many nights and told her she was beautiful. On his return from his evenings out with friends, he used to bring her fragrant cambeli bracelets bunched with tight, crisp buds; he took her to Lawrence Gardens on Sunday afternoons during winter, and once every month she went with him to see a film. But a whole year passed and each month her periods flowed freely and brazenly, until one month he said, "I think you should go and see the lady doctor in Mayo Hospital." "Yes," she murmured, her head bent low, the warm wetness burning like a fire between her thighs.

The lady doctor examined her. "There is nothing wrong, your periods are regular, you say, and your uterus is normal. Maybe your husband should have a checkup."

Salma couldn't tell him. He kept asking her and she answered, "It's God's will, the lady doctor said, everything was all right."

And he waited. Throwing himself on her, thrusting himself into her, he waited. And then he began to beat her. She knew he was punishing her for not being pregnant. Once he threatened he would get a new wife, someone who wasn't barren like her. She said, "It's not my fault, it's Allah's will." That angered him more.

Salma didn't mind the beating so much. He only slapped her, sometimes on the cheek, sometimes on the side of the head. Only once he pushed her against the door. That was actually her fault. He had wanted *maash* and, forgetting what he had requested, she cooked *chana daal* instead because her head was buzzing with too many sounds, and he lost his temper. She should not have said, "It's *daal*, what difference does it make whether it's *chana* or *maash?*" She saw a look of surprise on his face, then a wave of anger washed over it and he thundered, "Now your tongue is loosened, you barren slut!" And leaving the bed, kicking the tray with the food with his foot, he came to her and slammed her against the door. "Go back where you came from, you wretch!"

But that was before the notebook. And now he had found it.

He had come home earlier than usual. It was not even quite twelve as yet, and she was still writing down her newest couplet.

O drifting people of an unsettled world,
I will not share with you your dreams . . .

The spinach and meat stew was burning because she was too engrossed in writing. The acrid pungency of burnt meat and spices wafted into her nose just as her husband knocked. Slipping the note-book under the pillow on her bed, she dashed into the kitchen, poured water in the burning pot, turned off the stove, and then raced to the door.

"Where are you? It's not like this is some three-storied mansion and you have to come running down three flights of stairs." He came in, his bicycle making a clattering noise on the threshold as he pulled it into the brick courtyard.

"I was in the bathroom," she said, avoiding his gaze. "I was washing some clothes." And then her mouth opened and she heard herself say, "You're always so impatient. I'm here, I haven't run away."

He turned to look at her, as if she were not his wife, the same woman who opened the door to him every day, but someone else.

"What? Your tongue is out of control again, it seems." He looked tired, there were dark circles under his eyes and he seemed to be out of breath. "Give me some water," he said, and went off in the direction of their bedroom.

He was sick, she realized. Fever perhaps. Last night he had coughed until he was hoarse and when she got up to give him water, he had moaned as if in pain. Quickly she went off to get chilled water for him.

When she brought in the glass of water, she saw he had her note-book in his hand. He had opened it and she knew he had already read some of what she had written. She did nothing to stop him. Placing the glass on a small table next to his bed, she left the room and came and sat down on a chair on the veranda.

New knots formed in her head. Her mind sang with new verses, new formations reverberated in her ears like the musical notes of a sitar.

My eyes have seen too much anguish and pain,
I now long for a single moment of succor . . .

He came out with the notebook. His face was flushed, his eyes bulged and the skin on his dark, angular cheeks, tanned from cycling to work in the sun, was quivering and vibrating as if stirred from within.

"So this is what you have been up to, slut! For whom have you been writing these words, these . . . these words?" He advanced, tearing out page after page with a ferocity that made him stumble, made him falter on his feet.

The sun had moved to the other side of the veranda, and although she was not wearing her shawl, Salma did not feel the chill at all. The winter sky looked like a blue *dupatta* stretched taut and clean. Around her flies buzzed, a small sparrow alighted on the wall of the courtyard, hopped restlessly for a few seconds, then flew off. On the rose bush next to the wall of the courtyard, there were new flowers, diminutive, crested, ivory-white, like the white of notebook paper. A radio played outside the courtyard wall, a woman's voice surged in song to the beat of musical instruments Salma knew nothing about. Except the drum. That beat, like the beat of her own heart, was distinguishable. Into the song wove the street vendor's voice, echoing repetitively outside in the gulley, mingled with the voices of children shouting in a game of marbles. "Vegetables, fresh vegetables, very cheap today!" the *sabziwallah* was saying. She remembered the burnt spinach and wondered if she should stop him and get something else. Perhaps some cauliflower, crisp, with well-formed florets, round and full like a bouquet.

"You slut!" Her husband ripped the pages into shreds, calling her names, swearing until his face was bathed in sweat. The veins in his neck swelled and pulsed. Finally, throwing the notebook at her so that it fell in her lap like a wounded bird, he wiped sweat from his forehead and raised a fist. "You barren slut!"

Salma rose from the chair and pulled down the edges of her *kameez* with trembling hands. "I'm not barren," she said, adjusting the *dupatta* on her shoulders and pushing back a strand of hair that had come loose from her braid, "and if you hit me today, I will open that door and walk out into the gulley and you will never see my face again."

Although he was still standing before her, she did not see him or the shocked surprise on his face. Words formed a screen before her eyes, like rain coming down in a sheet of moisture on a windy day. Walking past him, she stooped to pick up, one by one, the torn, crumpled, soiled pages, and placed them between the cracked, twisted covers of the notebook.

The notebook snug under her arm, she strode briskly across the courtyard. "*Sabziwallah, O sabziwallah,*" she called out, opening the door, the words echoing in her ears like the refrain of a song. "You have any fresh cauliflower today?"

⊷⇒ History Lessons ⇐⊶

March is a popular month for floggings in the city. There's no heavy downpour to disrupt open-air events and the cricket season, having spent itself in rounds of victory and defeat and then victory again, is over. The revelry of *Basant* has also been and gone, although not without exacting a price. Listed in the local newspapers are reports of the usual mishaps involving fatal falls from roofs during lengthy kite-flying sessions; as one's keen eyes fixed themselves on the kite, which, heaving, mounted toward the clouds, no, even beyond them to the blue expanse of clear, unclouded skies, one went too far, close to the low parapet wall and, in another instant, over it. 'Rooftop accidents,' the caption in the newspaper reads. As for the weather, that too, calm and spring-like, lacking the savagery of summer heat and the cutting chill of winter, does not impel. People in the city must now look elsewhere for diversion, and the floggings, it seems, are just the thing to cure the passivity that follows at the heels of *Basant* and the cricket season euphoria.

In Shahid's history class too at Model High School, an infectious lethargy has set in. Kamal Ahsan, the most animated cricket enthusiast, has ceased rather abruptly to affect Imran Khan's celebrated swing, a skillful demonstration with which he had been amusing his classmates until recently. Today, he is contemplative. On several occasions that day Shahid has looked up from correcting notebooks to see the solemn-faced boy pensively tapping a pencil on one smooth, honey-brown cheek, his eyes fixed dreamily on the empty space before him, the assignment on his desk apparently forgotten.

Earlier, reading from their textbooks about the spectacular accomplishments of the great Moghul emperor Aurangzeb, the students exhibited no excitement whatsoever; the words describing Aurangzeb's religious zeal and his greatness as a leader fell from their mouths like a child's recitation of a famous poem—faltering and without meaning. They turned the pages of their history books wearily. They yawned.

Finally Shahid prescribed a written assignment in the hope that the hand and the mind, working together, might trigger some enthusiasm.

"Sir, are you going to the flogging at the Jail Ground?"

It is Kamal. His question catches Shahid off guard. He has been collecting the notebooks in which the boys have hastily scribbled thoughtless answers to questions about Aurangzeb's splendid reign, and as he pauses next to Kamal's desk, the boy transfixes his gaze upon Shahid's person, his head tilted to one side, long thick eyebrows arched inquiringly. There's a sparkle in his eyes. About to answer with an infirm "No," Shahid is engulfed by a feeling of relief when the bell rings. A clamor ensues, and the schoolmaster moves on.

An hour later, safely installed in the teachers' lounge, Shahid leafs through the newspaper which seems to be dominated by pictures of the President; his large, bloated face, with its deep-set eyes and the sculpted Sandhurst-style mustache, appears to have been photographed from every conceivable angle. *The master with the kohl-lined eyes*, is what people in the streets call him.

As he scans the headlines, Shahid wonders uneasily about Kamal's query. He realizes, with some guilt, that he's been troubled with feelings of petty curiosity since yesterday about the lashing, a feeling you do not admit to your students. Will the boy view his teacher's silence as a sign of weakness, will he sense in it his vacillation, his indecision? Tomorrow then, Shahid tells himself, why not talk about flogging in class, a lecture perhaps on the historical significance of establishing, on the eve of the twenty-first century, methods of punishment that are fifteen hundred years old?

Something in the newspaper catches his eye just as he finishes grappling with the issue of Kamal's question. "Crowd Sees Four Whipped," the heading casually informs:

At a local stadium in a small north-eastern town, four men were whipped last week before thousands of people. The lashings were ordered by a military court after the four were found guilty of escaping from jail. Each was sentenced to fifteen lashes, but two of them, Sikander Solangi and Ali Nawaz Solangi, fainted after the sixth lash. The whipping was halted at the advice of a doctor. While the lashing was in progress, Ali Nawaz Solangi, a ninth grader, started shouting slogans in which he was joined by the crowds. Before the whipping began, the city administration and the Martial Law authorities made arrangements to block every road and all traffic was checked by the police.

What had the boys done to warrant a jail sentence, and what slogans were they shouting? It couldn't have been "Down with the Martial Law authorities" or even "Down with the police." That would have guaranteed a more severe punishment; they might have been revived and brought back after an hour or two of rest for further lashing. *I hope somebody is writing all this down*, Shahid thinks, *not some faceless Harvard professor or some research-plagued political scientist who is interested in the whys and hows but not in actual accounts, the sum and substance of history, not a journalist either, because newspapers don't turn into history books. Who, then?*

Ghulam Ahmed, the science teacher who arrives in the lounge for afternoon prayers with the dedication of children gathering in the field for afternoon cricket, has finished praying and is now solemnly rolling his prayer mat. His head flung low, he's still mumbling something hurriedly under his breath. Shahid realizes, with a slight feeling of annoyance, that he is alone with Ghulam Ahmed at the moment. An unexpected impulse prompts him to hold out the newspaper toward his colleague.

"Well, now we're whipping ninth graders," Shahid says sharply.

Ghulam Ahmed takes the paper. His small round eyes are hidden under ponderous lids, and he has an annoying habit of never looking at you directly until it's absolutely necessary. He always looks sideways instead, as if addressing an unseen presence. Placing the mat on the upper shelf of an old, dusty bookcase which has not seen books as yet, he slowly eases his body into an armchair directly across from Shahid. A thick-palmed hand is lifted which he moves over his coal-black beard in a characteristic gesture that, Shahid is sure, results either from an unconscious need to conceal the unattractive appendage or flaunt it. He noisily flaps open the paper.

"Children must be taught the difference between right and wrong," he finally says, just as Shahid is about to give up on a response to his remark. His face disappears behind the newspaper. "They're going astray," the voice informs him authoritatively, "running after western values, wearing tight American jeans, destroying their morals by watching obscene films on the VCR and by listening to that American singer with a woman's face." The hand emerges to smooth out his crisp white cotton shirtfront and disappears again, to caress the beard no doubt.

Shahid doesn't wish to defend America, no, nor the American singer with the woman's face, but he can't let Ghulam Ahmed have the last word either. However, before he can order his thoughts and shape them into a coherent rebuttal, Ghulam Ahmed suddenly lowers the paper and faces Shahid squarely. To Shahid's surprise, he's actually looking at him directly. "I'm not surprised young boys are getting into trouble, not surprised at all," he says. He would be quite handsome without the straggly beard, Shahid thinks.

"But lashing school children?" Shahid exclaims testily, unable to modulate his tone. "Surely other forms of punishment, less extreme, can be chosen for the children." Shahid is not given to twitching or quaking when angered, nor does he raise his voice, but sometimes the science teacher says things that make him seethe inwardly and he feels, quite irrationally, a desire to yank the man's beard.

"My dear sir," Ghulam Ahmed says in an authoritative, controlled tone, "we have to discipline our children or else we will have a society of vagabonds and ruffians on our hands in a few years. How can we have learning without reinforcement? Huh?"

Did the 'we' refer to the class of teachers or did he mean 'we, the military government?'

"Aren't you familiar with the concept of behavior modification?" he is asking. "Rewarding what is good, punishing what is wrong?"

Ghulam Ahmed fancies himself as a true man of science. He had done his FSC in the hope of going on to medical school, but a third division blocked that venture. The stunted scientist in him never quite accepted defeat, however.

"I don't say one shouldn't reward good behavior and punish when there's evidence of wrongdoing, but lashing children?" Frustration makes Shahid repetitive.

"You see this, you see this?" Without warning Ghulam Ahmed's burly frame springs to life. Beads of sweat quiver like tiny balls of mercury on his forehead. He thrusts the paper into Shahid's hands and jabs a coarsely knotted finger at a heading. "Read this," he says, a triumphant glimmer appearing in his eyes.

Shahid takes the newspaper from him, sorry that he had started this discussion in the first place. His colleague might report him to the principal for speaking against the government's policies and, who knows, it might be Shahid getting whipped next.

"Porno Show in Jail." Shahid reads on. According to the report a school teacher was arrested on charges of obtaining a porno film and arranging a showing in jail. What an imbecile. Why have the showing in jail? Fifteen lashes for him, at least. For most minor offenses like shouting anti-government slogans, organizing strikes on campuses, writing and printing material that makes oblique references to the military government's show of gluttonous piety, throwing rocks at the police or the offices of the USIS or the American Consulate, for these and for crimes related to pornography, fifteen lashes are standard fare.

"Well sir, why are you silent? What do you say now, huh? How should this man be punished? Lashes are too good for him." Hanging then? In another instant Ghulam Ahmed would begin to gesticulate wildly with his hands, his dark brow furrowed solidly, his manner scornful, and then Shahid wouldn't know what to do.

"Yes, yes, just terrible," Shahid offers lamely, ready to give up. "Well, I must go now. Time for class."

On his way out Shahid bumps into Naseer Nawaz, a pleasant-faced young man who has recently joined the staff of Model High School as the new English teacher. He hopes to be a bureaucrat one day. Apologetically explaining his role as a teacher he said once, "One must eat, you know," and lamented the absence of any free time to prepare for the prodigious civil service exam.

"I'm off to class," Shahid says hurriedly, sorry to leave his young colleague alone with Ghulam Ahmed without warning him first. But he's not in a very charitable mood at the moment.

⋆⇒◉⟨═⋆⋆

As Shahid rides his bicycle down Ferozepur Road, vast and unruly waves of traffic hit him like a blinding dust storm. Uneven columns of Toyotas, Hondas and Datsuns separate and splice with rapid and precarious irregularity around him; towering, double-deckered, lopsided buses plod on wearily and with little thought to the bristling mass of traffic around them and suspended perilously from their entrances are men of all ages, most of them wearing deadpan, fatalistic expressions like trapeze artists in a circus. Pedestrians too, undaunted, filter through the maze created by cars, tongas, ox carts, and rickshaws. Having eyes in the back of one's head would help, especially when one is on a bicycle in the midst of this morass.

Finally, half an hour later, Shahid is on the Mall and in another fifteen minutes he finds himself approaching Tollington Market. Erected in 1864 by the British masters to house the Punjab Exhibition, the building, in its present dilapidated condition, provides a centrally located, convenient place for the moneyed to buy imported jams, jellies and soaps, also fresh fruit, grains, out-of-season vegetables, plump, well-fed chickens, beef, mutton and expensive fish. A small restaurant stuck into a corner is also a sanctuary for college students who gather here for trysts, coffee, club sandwiches, and bold, uninhibited talk. Shahid remembers with a smile how he had often spent the last five or six rupees in his pocket on coffee and sandwiches for Zarina with the dreamy eyes. He wonders where she is now.

As he takes his foot off the pedal at the traffic signal, Shahid notices military police on the footpath across from Tollington Market. The uniformed men are standing about with no particular sense of urgency, their eyes squinting in the afternoon sun, their dark, bushy mustaches glistening as though painted over with tar, their guns slung carelessly behind their shoulders as if they were only schoolboy satchels. People seem to be pressing forward expectantly, voices and sounds mingling and escalating. There must be a procession ahead. Women. Colored *dupattas*, dark *burkas*, long, trailing blanket-like *chadors*. The women are out to protest the *shariat* laws, to make loud noises about freedom, about rights.

Shahid decides to veer off in the direction of a side road and avoid the rush that's bound to ensue as the demonstrators become reckless, eventually getting too boisterous for their own good. There will be tear gas and stampedes and the inevitable baton-charge to contend with in a short time. He's already delayed. But a half hour spent in suffering an uphill detour won't make too much of a difference; nothing ever happens on time anyway.

The road Shahid has taken will ultimately lead him, albeit in a roundabout manner, to Lawrence Road and a right at the fork instead of a left would bring him face to face with Jail Ground.

⊶⊷⊜⊏⊷

Outside the east gate of the old jail is an irregular expanse of land, uneven and bereft of foliage. Its barrenness contrasts with the greenery of the park across the road where there are broad oaks and tall tahli thickly laden with spring growth, swishing about in the indolent March breeze, and where the grass gleams carelessly like a plush new carpet.

The hard-surfaced portion of land adjacent to the east wall of the jail, known as Jail Ground, is where, for reasons known only to the authorities, the public flogging is held.

The jail, wasting away like a famine-stricken body, was closed up after the internment of the fallen prime minister. Soon after he was hanged by the General's orders in the darkness of night in another place, the old jail was permanently shut down. Markets and housing developments have sprouted around it with the haste of an unhappy memory being put to rest. The decrepit building now stands like an uninhabited island, curiously out of place in its present surroundings, slowly but perceptibly falling apart. Unfortunately, it doesn't have the tenacity of Tollington Market.

Road hawkers are not permitted to bring their carts into the Ground, but there's no law against standing on its fringes. They are here today, in great numbers, their carts heaped high with fruit. There are tart, burnished-yellow tangerines, small bananas tightly crowding ten or twelve on a bunch, also early melons, apple-green and speckled. Orange rinds, banana peels, and hollowed half-moon melon slices will gradually pile in heaps around the vendors' carts as people rip open bananas, devour melons, and tear up orange after orange in a frenzy. The air will become redolent with a piquant aroma at once sweet and acrid.

There is time. Shahid installs himself at a table outside Rahman Cafe, a small tea shop in the middle of the sprawling cloth market where one can buy the best smuggled Indian silk, American georgette and chiffon. Situated at right angles to the Ground, the market has the advantage of overlooking the Ground from some height, thereby giving the observer an opportunity to look down at the proceedings.

From the murky interior of the shop issues the piercing treble of an old Nur Jahan song, which, like other such songs, has the uncanny ability of pumping one's heart with a sudden rush of sentimental rapture.

Love is young, beautiful is the world around us,
The heart has surrendered the treasure of joy.

"Tea, *sahib?*" The face of a child appears before him, the eyes those of a man, seasoned, hardened, canny. Like Kamal, Shahid's student.

"Yes, one set, and two pastries." The child nods, swooping down to run a wet, filthy rag over the table with the ease of an experienced dancer before moving away.

Minutes later the boy returns with a tray, a bleached white china cup teetering and clattering in its saucer as he sets the tray down. The pastry is ornamented with a wide, stiff layer of bright green icing studded with pink and yellow crisscrossing, like bands on a paper kite. The tiny round teapot, despite the cracks down its side, guarantees hot tea, steeped to a coppery red, promising to glide down the throat in one long, satisfying caress.

"Three-and-a-half rupees," the boy is saying, his gaze drawn to the Jail Ground. "There's going to be a flogging there," he points in the direction of the *maidan*. "There will be a large crowd soon. Last month they brought people over in trucks and buses." He waits patiently while Shahid counts the change and puts it on his small, open palm, throwing in something extra for him. The boy flicks the tiny, thin *chawani* expertly with his fingers and, playing with the grimy rag on his shoulder, leaves Shahid with his tea.

The pastry proves to be dry and the icing sticks to Shahid's palate tenaciously. He dislodges it with his finger. Abandoning the rest after the first bite, he gulps down the tea which doesn't disappoint. The tables in the area have filled up by now and a drone-like chatter of conversation about the same thing thickens like fog, interspersed with sounds of car horns, cries of children, and of course, the regulated, sing-song voices of hawkers advertising their wares.

Absently Shahid picks up his cup only to find there's no more tea left. The boy loiters nearby. He wants him to finish quickly and vacate the table for the next customer. Business is good today and the pastries keep coming. Shahid decides to walk down to the Jail Ground.

Following some unexpected evening showers, the city wears a bathed, cleansed look. The foliage, now washed, glows with an emerald light. The roads are a heavy gray color, almost black. Spring is a short-lived season in the city, with its quick spurt of color, so quickly gone that for most people the memory is like a longing only partially fulfilled. Shahid hastens his step.

The boy was right. A massive truck, floridly decorated with gaudy mirrors, bright paint and gilded flowers, laboriously plows down to the edge of the Ground. From its bowels, as if it were Noah's ark bringing its passengers to safety from the deluge, emerge men, young, old, dressed in the popular *shalwar-kameez* suits, only a few wearing pants and shirts. Many are young, lean-cheeked and sport hefty mustaches. Shahid realizes, perhaps for the first time, that it is rare to find a man nowadays in Lahore who doesn't have a mustache. His own had suffered on account of uneven trimming and had to be shorn. First a national dress, now a national face.

Accompanied by shouting that appears to draw parallel cheers from the bystanders on the other side of the road, the new arrivals make a dash for the *maidan*. This fresh surge of activity lends a certain frantic energy to the crowds around Shahid. Everyone is moving now. If he doesn't hurry he won't be able to find a suitable spot from which to observe the lashing.

As he weaves his way through the thickening crowd, Shahid is surprised he doesn't see a single face that looks even vaguely familiar. He had entertained the possibility of running into Ghulam Ahmed at least. But given the size of the throng, there's a chance he might not be spotted even if he is around.

At four, when the sun is gliding calmly toward the western horizon, two police jeeps with an army truck in tow roll down the main road, drive at a cautious speed past the fruit vendors and make a right turn on the road that runs between the park and Jail Ground. Slowly continuing onward, they finally make a screeching stop at the far end of the *maidan* where a brick driveway leads to the jail gates. Several policemen jump from the jeeps with dramatic litheness, batons held aloft like swords withdrawn from their sheaths. Leaving the police jeeps at the entrance to the driveway, the truck now begins to move again, lumbering noisily on the uneven surface of the driveway which is ridden with potholes wherever the bricks have crumbled. It comes to a standstill some yards away from the jail gates, which are rusty, corroded from age and disuse, and heavily padlocked.

All at once there is a revitalized exodus toward the ground from all directions. The inhabitants of the city, impatient with anything and anyone that threatens to impede their advance or slow them down, jostle and elbow and push and shove. Women, too, pick up speed, anxious it seems, not to be left behind. Drawing their *burkas* and *dupattas* about them closely, those with children straddled on their hips careless of where the *chador* or *dupatta* may be falling, they press forward eagerly.

Those already in the Ground scramble with disorderly haste toward the nucleus of the *maidan* as the prisoner, handcuffed, is helped out of the back of the truck. Shahid is still on the fringes of the *maidan*, his progress thwarted, it seems, by waves of men and women who move quickly and with electrifying vigor in the direction of the flogging center. Swallowed up in the throng of spectators, he can hardly breathe.

More time is lost as he fights to catch his breath. He is pushed back. Finally, when he's ready to resume the trek, he finds himself thrown against another wall of spectators. The crowd is dense, almost impenetrable, and reminds Shahid of the field of harvest wheat he had to stumble blindly through on his way to school as a child, always losing his way in it.

Unless he makes a retreat, and that too with speed, to the place the vendors are positioned, he may not be able to see anything at all. Laboriously, because going against the flow of the crowd is worse than going with it, Shahid trudges to the bank overlooking the Ground. This too is now lined solidly with more onlookers, who had perhaps, like him, failed to make it to the center of the arena.

Although it is a cool, windy afternoon, Shahid has begun to sweat and there's a taste of dust on his tongue. He's also thirsty. A man next to him is talking, laughing and eating an orange all at the same time, and when some moist seeds are spewed inadvertently onto Shahid's face he decides it's time to forego the history lesson. Anyway, from where he stands he can't see enough.

Most of the tables at Rahman Cafe are now vacant. The young boy, the shopkeeper's assistant, is nowhere in sight. But Nur Jahan's melancholy strains continue to radiate from the dark insides of the small shop.

> Let me hear your voice, where are you?
> Come, the night is on the wane.

Unlocking the padlock on his bicycle, Shahid walks away from the cycle stand, from Rahman Cafe, and the agitated murmuring of the crowd in the *maidan.*

> About to leave the sky is the caravan of stars,
> Where are you?

The melody follows him, like the diffused memory of happy times, of the game of *gulee danda* in the streets of one's childhood, of the taste of chilled *lassi* on a summer morning.

⊷≡◉⊂≡⊶

The report in the Urdu daily the next morning is detailed:

At the flogging yesterday, a crowd consisting of thousands of spectators was present. The road had to be blocked off and in the buildings surrounding the area, men, women, and children climbed on the rooftops.

Shahid peers closely at the picture of the crowd. *Is he in there somewhere?*

District Superintendent of Police of Naulakha, Syed Bedar Hasan, and also SHO Malik Abdul Rahim were accompanied by the district magistrate Syed Ali Ahmed Shahzad and Superintendent of the Jail, Muhammad Amir Khan. The jail doctor and a large police contingent were also present. As soon as the criminal, Ghulam Din, was removed from the police truck the crowd became restless. Ghulam Din was dressed in jail *khadar shalwar* and *kameez* and also wore a cap. A chair sat in the middle of the clearing and Ghulam Din was brought to it. The prisoner put both hands on the back of the chair and bent over. The jail doctor examined Ghulam Din and listened to his heart, and checked his blood pressure.

Would they have taken him back if his blood pressure had been high, or if his heart showed an abnormality?

After this one of the police officers read out the prisoner's offense. It should be remembered that Ghulam Din, a shopkeeper who sells dry fruits outside the shrine of *Daata Sahib*, has been charged with indecent behavior involving a young woman in his neighborhood.

Who saw them? A friend? A passerby?

Then, with the permission from the doctor and at the order of the magistrate, another prisoner came forward to administer the flogging. When he raised his arm high in the air, Deputy Superintendent of the Jail stopped him, saying that the lashes had to be administered according to the *shariah* law. Consequently the man giving the lashes administered them in such a way that his arm never rose above the level of his shoulder. This act was completed in a few minutes. During this time Ghulam Din continued to smile, and after the last lash he lifted both his arms high in the air and shouted "*Ya Ali!*" in an animated voice. At this point DSP of Naulakha, Syed Bedar Hasan, pinned him down.

Did he think he was Majnu, the legendary lover, or maybe a soldier engaged in battle, a fierce warrior of love?

Many of the people in the crowd attempted to talk to Ghulam Din, but he remained silent thereafter. He was subsequently taken back to jail. While the lashes were being administered, many people were heard to remark that the flogging was not real. One man said, "Even the dirt on his clothes has not been shed," while another said, "There were no welts." Some others were saying it would have been better if one of the police's own men had given the lashes. Another man said anyone can submit to a thousand lashes. During the course of the flogging the crowd threatened to get out of hand several times, but the police were able to control it.

Crowds. Like sheep. Pushed to violence, beaten to submission, so pliant, like sodden clay. Shahid is still scanning the newspaper when Ghulam Ahmed walks in for his mid-afternoon prayer.

"Have you seen this?" Shahid asks in an unnaturally loud voice, spit flying from his mouth to his surprise. He thrusts the paper at Ghulam Ahmed, his heart jabbing violently against his ribs.

"The flogging?" Ghulam Ahmed asks casually. "Oh, yes, I was there. Were you there?"

"Yes, I mean I was there, but I left before the horrible event began. Next we will be stoning women and after that . . . and after that . . ." Shahid stumbles, unable to continue. There's a buzzing sound in his ears, like the whirring of a knife sharpener, and he feels a wave of heat rising to his head.

"And after that, what, sir, a moral cleansing? Surely you see that coming, and you see that it must?"

"Moral cleansing? What do you mean?" Shahid gets up from his chair, folds the newspaper with forced calm and holds it tightly against his chest as if it were a shield.

Ghulam Ahmed unrolls the prayer mat. "The process of change that has been instituted," he begins speaking in a slow, measured tone, "will wash out moral decrepitude from our society. Such punishments as you saw yesterday, and yes, stoning too, if necessary, and cutting of hands, will usher in an era of reform for our people. We shall be an example of moral cleansing, yes dear sir, a lesson for the history books."

Shahid doesn't know exactly how it happens, but Ghulam Ahmed's head falls forward and while he struggles to free his beard, Shahid doesn't seem to feel his own hand, or the power that impels it.

⋅⋙ Shadows ⋘⋅

"Wear something bright and colorful," the old woman said, glancing up and down at Marium with only a small movement of her eyes. "And use a little makeup." She stretched her lips, revealing teeth eaten away by betel-leaf and tobacco. "So many nice things these days," she murmured, as if speaking to herself.

Marium's first reaction to the woman's suggestions was anger, silent, swift and mean, rankling in her throat like a cough held back in fear. Her mother, who was pouring tea in the woman's cup, turned to look at her and Marium suddenly realized she was being observed from Kariman's vantage point. Her anger returned, with it abhorrence for the woman who gulped her tea noisily and to whom her mother was now presenting the plate on which yellow cake slices precariously huddled together with sugar biscuits and a cream roll.

The woman's name was Kariman. Just Kariman. A matchmaker now, she was once a wife and mother. But times were hard. The children were gone, and she was alone, a widow, with no means of support. So she turned to matchmaking. Now, for a fair price, she brought families together and helped forge links between strangers.

It's a noble profession, Marium told herself after the woman had left. Where would the majority of the nation's girls be without assistance from the likes of Kariman? Only a handful could find their own grooms; others had to rely on the hard work and efforts of matchmakers. Marium became aware that her hostility toward the woman was misplaced. She was, after all, trying to find her a husband. Perhaps I'm not being fair, Marium thought as she threw out the swollen, sodden tea leaves in the trash and began rinsing the teapot absently.

But it wasn't easy to be fair. Kariman was only one of the many women Marium's mother had engaged in the last five years to seek out a fitting husband for her daughter. The search, fervent and arduous, had proven futile. Marium lacked the graces that brought eager families to the doors of young, unmarried girls. Her father, once a petty government officer, was now retired with a pension of a thousand rupees a month, and she was not beautiful, she was not even fair of complexion, even the polite 'wheatish coloring,' didn't apply to her. She was not like some of the other girls in the family who had been plucked, like ripe fruit off a tree, while still in their late teens or early twenties. The last one to go was Kausar, her uncle's youngest child, not quite eighteen yet.

Marium was fond of Kausar and had protested vehemently when she heard a good match had been found for her cousin.

"But Chachaji, she's only eighteen, you should let her finish F.A. at least," she argued with her uncle. "Wait another year, just until she takes her second year exam."

"Good proposals don't come every day," her uncle said firmly, wisely. "She's not going to work ever, and if she likes to study she can think about going back to college after she's married."

And Kausar didn't like to study.

"Marium Apa, what will I do with a degree? I hate exams anyway," Kausar told her laughingly when, after failing to convince her uncle, Marium tried to use her influence with her cousin during a tutoring session. Looking at her Marium realized that the young girl indeed belonged, not in a classroom, but in a house with at least four or five servants, a *begum sahiba* she should be, and she would mature without being fettered by the stress and anxiety of exams and text books; none of that to mar her initiation into womanhood. Her jasmine skin shone with the freshness of early morning dew, her eyes glistened with a restive sparkle, and her hair, black like the midnight sky, hung down her back in a long, thick braid. It was a face meant for rouge and *kajal*, a face destined to be admired and fondled, cherished and bejewelled. Yes, she definitely didn't belong in a classroom.

"Just think, Marium Apa, I'll never have to take another exam!" Kausar spoke with a childish lilt. Marriage was to be her teacher then, and Marium had no doubt she would prove an apt pupil.

Kausar's wedding would be the fifth in the family since Marium started teaching at the Lahore Divisional School. Two were first cousins on her father's side, one a second cousin, another her sister-in-law's younger sister, and now it was Kausar's turn. It wasn't herself Marium worried about. It was her mother. With each successive wedding in the family, her mother seemed to become more withdrawn, quiet and sullen. When she smiled and joined the other women in the family gossip sessions, her face was like a mask, every feature exaggerated, the smile sheepishly expansive, the eyes crinkled up apologetically at the corners.

Sometimes Marium wished they were not so close. She and her mother. Not so much in each other's hearts. In her mother's eyes she saw the same despair she felt dragging at *her* own spirits every now and then.

I wish I could go away somewhere, become a gypsy, roam in places where no one knows me and I could find, in some far-off place a man who isn't looking for dowries and beauty, who wants only love and passion. In a place where there will be no drawing rooms and no matchmakers, I will be whatever I want to be, I will sit or stand, or run or laugh, or sing or dance, and no one will tell me to be careful, to be cautious. This man will see the real me, to him I will reveal my otherness without shame or reticence, to him I will be beautiful.

But this was all silliness on her part. She could never run away. There was nowhere to go.

And how can I abandon my parents?

There was a time, the first year after her M.A., when a steady stream of visitors had graced their door. Mothers, aunts, and sisters of eligible bachelors came often, accompanied nearly always by loud-mouthed, over-zealous matchmakers. At that time there was little reason to be nettled by their presence. Actually, Marium had secretly welcomed these visits. As she sat with these women in the small, dark drawing room of their house, her body quivered with emotions she hadn't known before, her heart thrashed in her chest, her brow became wet with perspiration. Vignettes of another life, more compelling and exciting than this one, passed before her eyes. She saw a man's face, indistinct and nebulous at first, then slowly taking palpable shape. Dark hair, a mustache, a gentle hand, the fingers long, the nails well-defined, a voice dubbed in laughter, a strong scent of cigarettes . . .

But where are those images now?

Marium couldn't remember when exactly the illusions slipped from her grasp. Time raced by her so quickly, tangled up with events like marriages, births and deaths in the family, teaching, tedious routines. And here she was, thirty-one, still unmarried, preparing for Kausar's wedding. Kausar, only eighteen, a young girl anxious to be bride and wife, impatient with waiting, adventurous, so eager to forsake the security of her parents' home for a new life with a man she knew nothing of except what she had been told piecemeal by sisters, aunts, cousins. She was brave. So completely steeped in the spirit of the adventure that awaited her, fearless, her vision uncluttered by farsightedness.

"Marium Apa, how can anyone be good at math?" she asked, her eyes impetuous and daring. She shook Marium's arm, then banged her notebook on her forehead.

Feigning seriousness, Marium wagged a finger of warning at her. "Now stop this nonsense Kausar. Do you want your husband to think you were so stupid you couldn't even pass first year? Now, pay attention. The trapezium . . ."

Kausar wailed. "A trapezium! The name is enough to give anyone a fever. Can we do this tomorrow, yes, yes, yes."

Acute angles, obtuse angles, logarithms and trapeziums—what are these to the poor girl?

"All right. But if you fail, don't blame me for it. Your fiance is an engineer, after you're married he'll know right away your math is hopeless and he'll never give you the household accounts. You'll always be begging him for money."

"I promise I won't fail, Marium Apa. Now tell me, what are you wearing at my *mehndi?*"

Something bright and colorful.

And now, after a long absence, Kariman was back. Marium knew her mother had sent for her, although she pretended to be surprised and looked at Marium as if saying, 'Oh this woman! Why doesn't she leave us alone?' when Kariman walked in with the news she was bringing some people over on Sunday. Kariman hadn't changed too much in five years. She still broke into fits of laughter that generally developed into coughing fits in no time, and she still devoured sweets greedily. Marium had been irked by her presence that morning.

The woman is here to dig up embers, rake a fire that has gone cold and will not smolder again. Will Amma never give up?

Once, a year ago, Marium's colleagues at school had tried to fix her up with a student's father, a widower. He was in his early forties, held an important position in the Ministry, and was anxious to marry again. "For the sake of his daughter," Mrs. Ahmed said, "but we know that's only half of it. The poor man's lonely and needs a woman by his side." And so Marium was to be presented as a prospect.

While Marium and Mrs. Ahmed stood on the front veranda of the school, he was to come up to them and engage Mrs. Ahmed in a conversation about his daughter's progress in her English class. Marium was to be introduced and subsequently the two would have an opportunity to observe one another.

The man arrived as scheduled. After a perfunctory glance at Marium, he began an earnest dialogue with Mrs. Ahmed about his daughter. Poor, diligent Mrs. Ahmed wasted no time in introducing her colleague and made several attempts to draw her into the conversation that seemed to have assumed a life of its own. From grades, it wavered to class behavior, from there to the school play, *The Merchant of Venice*, and on and on. All this time Marium, except for minor contributions like, "Yes, that's right," "No, I don't think so," "Yes, we must," etc., said little. Finally, after what seemed to her like long drawn hours of inattention, she mumbled "Excuse me," and walked away from them.

Later she was scolded by Mrs. Ahmed.

"Where did you run off to? He was asking about you after you left. I think he liked you."

That was the only time in the last five years that Marium had allowed herself to hope. And she bitterly regretted her slip afterward.

If he liked her, where was he? No doubt he has gone after jasmine cheek and lustrous eyes, after hair that flows like the midnight sky, after loveliness and youth.

Well, why not? If one seeks excellence in the things one buys, why not look for it in a wife? Don't you pick up mango after mango, hold it close to your nose, smell it, feel it for tightness or softness, look for any telltale brown spots that might betray overripeness, and then haggle over the price after the selection has been made?

Like forgotten fruit, she had been left out in the sun too long and had shrivelled up, like overripe mangoes that are not taken off the branches in time, she had developed brown spots which spoke of hopes soured and finally laid to rest. But she had cast out anchors and now hung, however precariously, by the lives of those with whom she shared her life; her parents, her cousins, her brother and his family, Kausar. Jealously she guarded her place.

Why is Kariman back?

Others had accepted the irrevocability of her situation. Her uncle no longer looked at her with that pitying smile he had reserved for her, her aunt had stopped telling her to dye her hair, and even her cousins, those who were her age and had daughters and sons in school, even they had ceased badgering her about the dull colors she wore, about her baggy *kurtas* and her long, wide cotton *dupattas*. Her father, too, had come to terms with her presence in the house. He was almost happy to have her around still, she thought.

Why does Amma persist?

She couldn't bring herself to ask her mother for details of the visit on Sunday and none were offered. Mother and daughter were in the kitchen, the one place where they were always the most communicative. Today silence hung between them like a thick, unwieldy curtain.

"Bring some fruit on your way home tomorrow," her mother finally said. Her back was to Marium, and she noisily clanked a ladle in a pot on the stove.

What is she cooking?

"Hmm." Marium mumbled, fighting the anger that was like a bitter, acrid taste on her tongue. How delicious to hurl to the floor in one clean, uninhibited motion the china cup Marium had just washed, a fragile cup on which a dash of indeterminate color was all that remained of the original flowered motif.

Moving away from the stove, her mother sat down on a low stool and started kneading dough in a large, blackened pan. Her arms and hands worked furiously with the dough, and she moved back and forth in a slow, dull rhythm, her head bent, a strand of hair falling across a cheek like a scar.

Marium set down the cup gently in the drainer and left the kitchen.

⊷≡◉≡⊷

First the moisturizer. Marium rubbed it over her cheeks in a slow circular motion. Her skin became taut with each pull, then slackened, the lines falling neatly into place like the edges of a puzzle. Her face glowed from the pressure of the massage and for a few seconds, warmed by the momentary gleam on her face, she held her head still, tilted to one side, and examined herself in the mirror.

How nice I look.

But the flush ebbed quickly. As the pallor of her skin returned she reached out for the stout, muddy-pink bottle containing the liquid makeup. None of this was familiar; the liquid makeup, the eyeliner, the rouge, the mascara, she hadn't used any of these things before.

Actually, it was dear Mrs. Ahmed's doing that she was experimenting this evening. Marium remembered a conversation that had taken place in the teachers' lounge only last week. Miss Younas, slim, well-attired, just out of college with a gold medal in political science and now teaching Pakistan Studies to the senior classes, was recommending Max Factor to Mrs. Ahmed. The latter had been complaining her brand left her lips caky and dry when Marium walked in on the conversation. Marium wondered if it was fair to blame it all on the lipstick. Mrs. Ahmed was nearing fifty and already the skin around her cheeks and under her chin had begun to corrugate.

"But the oldest brands are still the best," Miss Ahsan, another colleague, offered in a tone which implied serious expertise. "I've been using Max Factor for years and I've never had problems." Leaning toward Mrs. Ahmed with a small, pink palm resting on her right cheek, she said, "Just look at my face, see how smooth my skin is. And you can't tell I have foundation on, can you?" Miss Ahsan was in her early twenties and taught English. Recently she had become engaged to her cousin who was a doctor and had proclaimed without the slightest hint of regret soon after the engagement ceremony that she intended to give up teaching after marriage. "Afzal doesn't want me to work," she announced happily to her colleagues.

Both Mrs. Ahmed and Miss Younas had leaned forward to examine the cheek so generously proffered for examination. Both appeared impressed. Marium, who sat some distance away correcting notebooks, had remained silent through all of this since she had no opinion on the matter, and no experience either. But her curiosity had been piqued.

Yielding to an impulse a half an hour later, she cautiously approached Mrs. Ahmed, who was closest to her.

"Do you think foundation can help with blemishes on the skin?" Her fingers rose tentatively to touch her cheek and stayed there nervously.

"Why, yes, of course, particularly if it's the right shade."

"What shade do you think would be right for me?" Marium asked in a voice that seemed not her own.

"Medium, I'd say, Marium. There's a shop in Anarkali at the corner where Bano Bazaar begins, just before Zeenat Cloth Market. He has a good stock of foreign cosmetics." Mrs. Ahmed offered advice generously.

Marium scooped out some cream from the bottle with the tip of her forefinger, disturbing the perfectly smooth surface which was glossy and unmoving like early morning mud after a night of rain. She placed some under each eye, then tried to spread it evenly. But quickly the thick, creamy mixture became unwieldy.

Oh God! What have I done!

She was frightened by the effect she saw reflected in the mirror. The once darkened patches under her eyes were now a muddy white. Her face looked like a mask, at once grotesque and spectral. Taking a handkerchief from one of the drawers in her dresser, she hastily began wiping her face, rubbing the whitened areas until her raw skin throbbed painfully. But the muddiness would not be diminished. Instead, it spread down to the level of her cheeks, making her look ghoulish.

She realized she must wash her face.

I must not be so impetuous, so hasty, this time I must use the cream sparingly, a little bit only, a dab.

Slowly she smoothed it out, noting with some satisfaction that the effect was indeed becoming. The shadows were almost undiscernible, and gone too was some of the drabness of her complexion.

Now the eyes. Feeling confident just as she did in class, she pulled out a fine point brush from the slim, sleek bottle labelled 'Eyeliner.' When she tried to draw a fine line with it over her right eyelid she discovered her hand was shaking. She, who drew concave polygons and convex polygons, isosceles and scalene triangles with swift, sure movements of her hand on the blackboard every day, she couldn't keep the eyeliner in place. Twice the minute point of the brush strayed beyond the curve along her lashes. When she tried to wipe off the unwanted blackness she succeeded only in converting it to dark smudges. Her arm ached from the awkward position in which she had been holding it as she fussed with the eyeliner. *Uff!* She threw down the brush on the dresser in exasperation and leaned back wearily.

Like shots from an old black-and-white film, the scenes to be enacted this evening raced before her eyes.

The women are seated in the drawing room. They chat ceremoniously. Kariman is sprawled on a sofa next to Amma, her heavily jowled face frequently breaking into a laugh. Her eyes dart alertly back and forth. The guests, all women, mother, sisters, perhaps an aunt of the bachelor in question, are restless and fidgety, their gaze traveling around the room as if taking stock. And Amma, calm as always on the exterior, a storm of anxiety rising and billowing in her head until I too feel stifled by it. I enter with a trolley set with tea, cake, cream rolls and some fruit. Greetings are exchanged. I sit down. Kariman leans her bulk forward boisterously and asks me a question. Something casual, insignificant. "What do you teach, daughter?" An awkward silence interspersed with some awkward conversation ensues. Finally I leave the room with a politely murmured, "I forgot the sugar."

The foundation! Of course. She could use some to eliminate the dusky smudges on her eyelids. Straightening up in the chair where she had slumped for nearly ten minutes, Marium moved excitedly to the edge of her chair. The round, stout bottle of foundation lay open invitingly. The creamy moistness into which she dipped her finger seemed cold to the touch, like the surface of an earthen pitcher on a January morning. With extreme care, she gently deposited tiny dabs on the areas where the streaked liner had left an untidy murkiness. Next she started rubbing the dabs to even out the cream. Her skin glowed.

How easy, how simple, how simple this is.

She gazed at her reflection in the mirror, overcome suddenly by a surge of feeling that coursed through her body like a current. Her flesh tingled. Her hands began moving rapidly and she scooped out more foundation for her cheeks, painstakingly easing the viscous consistency into silky smoothness. Her face stared at her from the mirror like the face of someone she didn't know. The skin was luminous. A jasmine hue.

Something bright and colorful it was to be then. Her red suit, the one she was to wear at Kausar's wedding. Red had always been a good color for her, but of late she shied away from it. A bride's color, the color of desires that leapt up like flames inside you and then burnt themselves out only too slowly, leaving behind red, glowing embers. She drew the shirt over her head carefully so she wouldn't smudge any of her makeup.

Next, the hair. With swift sure movements she began combing her long, fine, hair, some of the silver strands flying about like errant kite strings. Up and down the comb went, as though driven by a magic force. Long, dark and shiny, her hair was soon curtained over her shoulders in inky darkness. So beautiful, a thing of pride.

⋯⇒◉⇐⋯

The conversation died abruptly when the women saw her coming through the door with the trolley. They smiled. All eyes turned to her. The room was badly lit as most drawing rooms, being so rarely used, are. Because she was bending over the trolley, not much of her face was visible. Cups and saucers rattled noisily as the trolley was maneuvered over the uneven portion of the threshold. The trolley in place, Marium lifted her face and murmured greetings.

The women—Kariman, her mother, the guests—gasped, their

smiles frozen. Before them stood a woman, tall and willowy. Her black hair was curtained over her shoulders in inky darkness. Her face was ashen and chalky, like the color of clean, pure mud after a night of rain. Her eyes were heavily ringed with *kajal*. The face was like a mask, at once grotesque and spectral.

"I've forgotten the sugar," she said, her voice reduced to a hoarse whisper.

⊷ Master ⊶

News of momentous events in the world of grownups trickled down to the children piecemeal. Sometimes they picked up threads from the ending of a story, and went back, bit by bit, faltering, bridging gaps, weaving a story. Snatches of conversation, expressions on the faces of a despondent aunt or a disgruntled uncle, a grandparent's scowl—the children used all this to make sense of what they heard. Often, they needed to pay special attention to crying or sniffling, anger, and unusual silences. However, despite the fact that Samina, who was the oldest among the children, kept a close watch on what was going on, the whole story rarely presented itself, mainly because every story unfolded in an interminably long and tortuous fashion and often seemed to have no precise beginning or end.

On this particular day, an afternoon when the summer sun was high and overbearing, the shades had been drawn, and the whirring of ceiling fans created a melancholy drone, Samina overheard her aunt and older cousin talking with their heads together. Aunt A. was saying that 'he' was not known to consume more than one medium-sized whole wheat *roti* every day, nor did 'he' defecate, and although 'he' had a woman with him whom the disciples called Bibi, 'he' didn't sleep with her the way men sleep with their wives. In short, 'he' was a holy man.

"What's a holy man?" Sakina, who had turned ten in June and was also eavesdropping, asked.

Propped up against soft, thin pillows on a *charpai* not too far from where Aunt Abida was ridding herself of the burden of this bizarre disclosure, Samina had been reading aloud to her younger sister the story of the princess housed in the belly of the pomegranate flower.

She tried to explain. "A holy man is like a saint, a man who, who . . . er . . . a man who is very religious."

"Like Dadajan?" Sakina tilted her small head questioningly.

"No, no, Sakina," Samina shook her head in ire. Their grandfather was a religious man, but certainly not a saint. "Dadajan is not a saint. Just saying prayers and fasting doesn't make you a saint."

"So what else does he have to do?" Sakina persisted.

"He has to give up worldly things and has to have a special bond with Allah, you know, he's closer to Allah than ordinary people." Samina knew she could never satisfy Sakina simply because in her, too, firsthand knowledge about holy men was scant.

"So he's a prophet?"

"Oh no, silly, don't you remember the *kalima*, 'There's no God but Allah and Muhammad is his prophet'? There can be no more prophets after our prophet."

"So who is he then?"

"Well, just a *dervish*," Samina pulled out a word from her repertory of big words and phrases. "Remember that word, all right? Now be quiet and don't ask any more questions."

That evening, while Samina was still attempting to untangle the configuration of what she and her sister had heard earlier in the day, she saw Aunt Maman, the oldest among her father's sisters, weeping quietly with her nose in her *dupatta*. She made sad noises like a bewildered child lost in the woods. Apa Najma, who was Aunt Maman's eldest daughter and was in her second year at Fatima Jinnah Medical College, sat nearby clenching and unclenching her teeth and muttering angrily under her breath. Every now and then she rounded a fist and banged it on her knee. Aunt Abida, meanwhile, who was only a year or so older than Apa Najma, looked ready to burst into tears herself.

Unfortunately, the younger girls always came upon a scene when it was halfway through or about to end, and that was no one's fault but their own. There were too many things to distract them: Zeenat, the cleaning girl, had stories to tell of her new lover, Masood Sahib; Dadima was reading the *Heer Ranjha* story and who would want to miss the melodrama of Heer's ill-fated romance with the flute-playing Ranjha? And then there was always some cousin or the other with whom news had to be exchanged. Of course, in those days the girls knew little or nothing about putting things in their proper order.

After supper, during a meeting between Abba, Amma, the grandparents, and Aunt Abida, Uncle Shah's name came up. Uncle Shah was what Samina and her sister called Apa Najma's father. He was being berated. In fact, everyone in the room, with the exception of Samina and Sakina, seemed ready to banish him from the family. Samina liked him. He always brought her children's books and magazines when he came to visit, and he also listened to classical music on the radio while he stayed at their house. Sometimes, drumming his fingers on the table to keep a *tabla*-like beat, he closed his eyes while listening to a mystifyingly complex raga, moving his head from side to side as if he were in a trance the whole time. Samina couldn't imagine how he had suddenly turned into such an odious person.

With her back to Aunt Abida, Sakina was playing with her doll while Samina pretended to be engrossed in a story from *Khilona*, the children's magazine that she was now getting bored with. Even though she was a tall and gangly fourteen-year-old with broad shoulders and two long, ropy braids dangling awkwardly on either side of her head, and even though she tended to stand out in an assembly of younger girls, no one seemed to take note of her presence this time. She and Sakina heard everything. It seemed most of their elders weren't even aware the children knew what was passing between them.

Dadajan swore heavily. "That man ought to be whipped," he roared, "I should just go and put a bullet through his chest." Dadajan's face had turned the color of a terra cotta pitcher, his eyes bulged, and a groove on his forehead jutted out thickly like a low mud wall.

"No Abbaji, we have to deal with this calmly, Maman's future is involved, she has four children, one a grown daughter, another a teenage son, how will she manage without a husband by her side?" Abba spoke in an unruffled voice, the kind he reserved for his children when he wanted to sway them to his way of thinking.

"I'm still alive, she can stay here as long as I'm alive. What is that bastard going to give her except sorrow and misery? I lament the day I accepted his match. He is a scoundrel." Spent after this outburst, Samina's grandfather leaned back wearily in his chair.

"Perhaps," Abba continued, "but we must at least try for a reconciliation. Let's hear his terms before we make any rash decisions."

Slowly a picture began to emerge. Aunt Maman's husband had become associated with a holy man simply called Master. As a result of this association, he not only spent the greater part of his time at Master's residence, he also surrendered much of his salary each month to him. Master, Samina fathomed, was the 'he' of the earlier exchange between Aunt Abida and Apa Najma. Aunt Maman had brought her dilemma to her parents (Dadajan and Dadima), and her brother (Abba), which explained why she was in Lahore in the middle of October; usually she came to spend a few weeks at their house either in the summer or around Christmas holidays. Samina was puzzled to see her, and surmised that she missed Apa Najma and decided to visit her on an impulse. Since there was no medical college in Sialkot, Apa Najma attended Fatima Jinnah Medical College for Women in Lahore.

Abba finally convinced Dadajan that Uncle Shah be given another chance.

"Why don't you go with him a few more times to this place when he asks you to, see what's going on, maybe you can gain his confidence by doing as he says for a while." Abba explained all this to Aunt Maman in a quiet, deliberate way, so she wouldn't think he was coercing her. "What do you think?" he asked.

"I'm fated to suffer, I know, I can see my children will have no home, they will be the object of pity and . . ." Aunt Maman slapped her forehead with her palm, broke down, and started weeping uncontrollably.

As if on cue, Aunt Abida, who had maintained a stoical silence all this time, came to her sister's side, put her arms around her and began crying as well with her *dupatta* held up to her face. Samina could see Dadajan getting redder and redder in the face. There was no doubt in her mind that if he were not so old and not suffering from a weak heart, he would have gone off to kill Uncle Shah.

Anyway, Aunt Maman, who, it seemed to Samina, resembled Dadima more and more each time she saw her, and particularly now, returned to her wayward husband. But before she left she said to Samina in a voice that didn't seem to have anything to do with the woman who had wept bitterly only the day before, "Come and spend winter holidays with us in Sialkot." Sakina, being younger, was always reluctant to go anywhere without Amma, so no one ever asked her; she usually stayed behind while Samina traipsed off to visit aunts and uncles during summer and winter holidays.

"Najma will be coming, you should come with her," Aunt Maman advised her, "and stay as long as she does, two weeks, all right?"

Samina secretly hoped that during her stay in Sialkot she would get an opportunity to accompany Uncle Shah and his family when they visited Master's house and perhaps see Master in person. Also, she was excited at the thought of seeing Kamil, Apa Najma's younger brother, for whom she nursed an undisclosed emotion which she hesitated to call love simply because it was entirely one-sided. About four years older than Samina, he had never paid her the slightest bit of attention. But that wasn't a concern; it thrilled Samina just to be around him.

Already she had written a poem in English about her undying, unrequited passion:

> I'll wait for you till the sun goes down,
> I'll wait until the stars come out,
> I'll wait for you till the leaves turn brown,
> I'll wait until you feel no doubt.

On the first day of Christmas holidays, Apa Najma and Samina got on the early morning train to Sialkot. They were in a third class compartment crammed with squealing, tired children, and men and women who seemed to have no connection with one another; husbands were quite unrecognizable as husbands except when their wives opened up tiffin carriers and handed them brown, butter-laden *parathas*. Samina and her cousin had also brought their *parathas*, cooked with a filling of spicy potatoes and minced meat.

As they rolled the bread and chewed off morsels, Apa Najma told Samina how much she would like to prove that Master was a fraud, a miscreant who was out to squeeze money from unsuspecting disciples. Of course, she was a medical student who carved up cadavers expertly, and studied dead fetuses and inert gray brains stored in large greenish-colored glass jars. Samina had accompanied her to her college once and watched from a distance as she and her classmates peeled skin off meticulously and artfully from what looked like a leg. She had thought, admiringly, anyone who had the courage to do this could do anything.

"But Apa, are you sure he isn't really a holy man?" Samina asked anxiously between chews.

"A holy man doesn't force people to turn their backs on their wives and children." Apa Najma replied, setting her teeth down firmly on the mouthful of *paratha*, a fierce look emerging in her eyes.

"But Buddha did that. He left his wife and his home and became an ascetic." Samina offered her comment wisely.

"Well, this man is no ascetic, no *dervish*, and he has a wife who is with him all the time, and he lives in great comfort, and expects everyone to bring in donations. And all this nonsense that he doesn't defecate . . . such rubbish! Perhaps he's constipated!" Apa Najma broke into a laugh and soon the two of them were so giddy with laughter they had to stop eating for a while.

Finally, since everyone was staring at them disapprovingly (particularly the women), they returned solemnly to their *parathas*, gazing at the speeding wheat fields and low mud houses outside their window, silently munching, both lost in their own thoughts.

Afterward they spoke in whispers. Apa Najma explained. "He just has some power over his followers, a hypnotic power." She looked serious, as if she were talking not to Samina who was only a young girl, but to a discerning adult. "And the idiots believe everything he tells them. Master, my foot! He's a villain."

Samina was not as foolish as she sometimes looked. She had seen people being hypnotized in films; as a matter of fact she had sneaked Dadajan's watch and chain from his coat pocket one afternoon while he took a nap, and tried to hypnotize Sakina. She kept dangling the watch in front of her sister's eyes until her wrist ached, but nothing happened. Sakina kept asking, "When will I get sleepy?" Finally, as Samina slipped the watch back into its place, she decided that was just a camera trick she had seen on screen.

"He hypnotizes people?" Samina asked curiously.

"No Samina, I mean he just has the ability to make people listen to him and do as he says." Apa Najma dismissed the whole question of hypnosis with a wave of her hand.

"But how are you going to prove he's a fraud, Apa, he has so many disciples." Suppose he hypnotized Apa Najma?

"I don't know yet, Samina, but I'm giving it some thought, you just wait and see." She had that same determined, intent expression Samina saw on her face when she was dissecting her cadaver.

⋅⇌◎⇋⋅

How surprised Samina was when Kamil actually spoke two complete sentences in greeting her.

"So how is Lahore?" he asked, with a smile.

"It's all right," Samina replied, blushing and wishing she could come up with a witty remark or an intelligent one at least. "We haven't had any rain yet and it isn't so cold."

"And what have you brought us from Lahore this time." Again the smile. Kamil was tall, and under long eyebrows, his eyes revealed nothing of what he was thinking. How Samina longed to drown herself in those dark, secretive eyes. Sometimes, when his hair was awry and he had a brooding look on his face, he reminded Samina of a picture of Lord Byron she had seen in one of Aunt Abida's literature books.

Of course she had brought five boxes of Nice biscuits, a large gunny bag fat with basmati rice, which was Dadima's special gift for Aunt Maman, also one large cloth bag bursting with several pounds of white sugar, and from Amma five yards of the finest sheer *malmal* for *kurtas* for the boys, and five yards of brightly printed polyester for a suit for Apa Najma's younger sister. Samina's suitcase had been filled up with all the gifts so that she had to carry a separate bag for the sugar and the biscuits. But what interest could Kamil have in basmati rice and white sugar? If only she had some other exciting things in her suitcase for him. Sweets perhaps, or maybe a Mont Blanc fountain pen.

If there had been some way of doing it without appearing utterly immodest, brassy and shameless, Samina would have told Kamil she had a special gift for him, a poem that she carried in her head. No, unfortunately, she didn't have Apa Najma's nerve.

Uncle Shah came home late that night so Samina didn't get to see him, and the next morning he left for work while she was still asleep. The day after, however, was Sunday and they all met for a lengthy breakfast. Putting his newspaper aside, Uncle Shah got up from his chair to hug Samina when she came in and asked if everyone in Lahore was well and then said, "Sit down." To Aunt Maman he said, "Give the girl a *paratha* and omelette Maman, she must be hungry."

Secretly Samina was expecting to see a change in him, a stamp of his association with a holy man, a man of God. She didn't know what exactly it was that she thought she would see, perhaps an air of detachment, a pious scowl, a long, straggly beard at least, a change of dress? Shouldn't he be wearing a large, woollen shawl around his shoulders, over a cotton *kurta* and *shalwar*, and also have a cotton cap on his head? He wasn't a bit changed. The same pleated khaki pants, white shirt with the sleeves rolled up, a woollen vest with a cable design which she had seen Aunt Maman knitting for him last year. He was clean shaven. Not even a mustache had been permitted. What a relief!

Samina was sorry that they were all supposed to dislike him now. Remembering Dadajan's anger especially proved unnerving, and she smiled guiltily, like a thief who had been caught. Glancing up at Apa Najma, Samina noted how she seemed to be concentrating on her *paratha* and tea with an intentness that was surprising, while Kamil, too, was taking enormous bites from the *paratha* on his plate and slurping tea from a large mug with an air of complete nonchalance, and Rahil and Seema, (the younger of Aunt Maman's children), happily tossed a piece of bread back and forth as if it were a ball. Sitting next to an oil stove, Aunt Maman was busy rolling out the *parathas*, and the whole room was filled with a warm, rich aroma of butter, cooked dough and thick, milky tea. Samina decided to ignore the awkwardness that she had experienced on first coming into the room, and plunge into the hearty breakfast that she always was so fond of.

That evening they all went to Master's *darbar*.

--+=≡◎◎≡+--

The bungalow was like any other generally seen in the older parts of town, aging, crumbling, a great many rooms scattered about here and there, a large courtyard in the middle bordered by a veranda, outside a fairly spacious lawn, thick with overgrown trees, eucalyptus, mulberry, an oak. Cluttered grape vines with knotted, coiled branches tenaciously climbed the sides of the house every which way, while thorny rose bushes growing with wild intemperance crowded the front of the high-roofed porch.

Inside, long, white, narrow tablecloths had been arranged in rows in the red-brick courtyard. Shiny stainless steel plates, jugs of iced water and glasses were in place. Those who had arrived early were already seated at the tablecloths crosslegged or on their haunches, some drinking water, others simply waiting either for food or for Master, Samina wasn't sure which at this time. The women were middle-aged and young, in *chadors* and *burkas;* there were men too and young boys with green stubble and fuzzy mustaches; a few teenagers and some of the men were dressed in pants and long-sleeved shirts, while others wore *shalwar* and *kameez* and coats.

The women were at separate tablecloths, although Samina was surprised to see they were not in another room, in *purdah* from the men. Conversations were being carried out in hushed tones, the men were not laughing or making jokes the way they generally do when they congregate. However, no one was saying prayers, and Samina saw no prayer rugs lying around for the faithful.

Uncle Shah disappeared within moments of their arrival, so that Samina, Aunt Maman, and Apa Najma and her younger sister and brother had to find their own away to the ladies' tablecloth. But Aunt Maman had been here before and she led them, Rahil and Seema somewhat subdued, Kamil staying behind at least three feet as if he didn't want anyone to know he was with the women, and Apa Najma tightly clutching her *dupatta* around her, her face carved into an expression of distaste as she grasped Samina's hand tightly and looked straight ahead.

After they sat down Samina realized that there was a steady trickle of people going to and from the room at the far end of the veranda, like a line of ants busy with purpose. Standing outside the entrance were some ten or twelve men (among them Uncle Shah), Samina noted, who whispered solemnly to each other and stayed away from the lines that were in motion. Of course it was clear that Master and his companion were in that room and all these people were going in to offer respects and whatever else it was they offered to him.

Suddenly Uncle Shah's group came to life, the lines dispersed, quickly transforming themselves into a shapeless crowd instead that seemed to be heaving as if powered by some unseen force. Everyone stood up and craned their necks. Samina felt her skin getting hot and cold with excitement. Her stomach contorted. She was to see a holy man in person and she might even have the opportunity of observing him at close quarters.

He was unmistakable. Dressed in a black shirt and *shalwar*, he walked unhurriedly, taking slow measured steps. There was the dark, woollen shawl draped on his shoulders, the beard was long, inky black and neat, no straggling here, and although he wore no cap, his hair fell down nearly to his shoulders like a woman's, and there were bead necklaces, onyx, tiger's eye and green jade, around his neck. He reminded Samina of the black-robed fakir who, appearing every summer, roamed on their street, sometimes singing devotional songs in front of their house. He would raise his loud, thunderous voice to the accompaniment of the clanking of long, blackened tongs whose metallic bars he rapped together rhythmically with a vigorous movement of his knotted, bony fingers.

From the fingers of Master's right hand dangled a *tasbih*, the beads a pale greenish-white. And, contrary to Sakina's expectations, he didn't scowl; he smiled benevolently at all those who pressed forward eagerly to kiss his hand. Samina felt something then, like a warm current coursing her body, a feeling that seemed to propel her, like the others, to touch Master's hand.

Apa Najma pulled her back. "Thief, villain, scoundrel!" She muttered in Samina's ear, as if she had sensed her weakness.

"Shhh . . ." Aunt Maman cautioned with a gesture.

And right beside him, like a queen, was the woman people called Bibi. She was wearing a green silk suit, a heavily embroidered Kashmiri shawl covered her upper body, her hair was knotted in a bun, and swinging from her ears were the longest earrings Samina had ever seen. Gold, no doubt, and surely studded with precious stones, swaying and dancing, caressing her long white neck as she turned her head to look this way and that, smiling, raising her hand to her forehead in *salaams* to the women who edged closer, anxiously waiting to touch her.

Before long everyone settled down on the tablecloths. Master and Bibi had moved to the seclusion of the shaded veranda and were now seated on a small rug of exotic design, their backs resting against silver-tasseled, green velvet pillows. A few men, two of whom reminded Samina of thugs in an Indian movie, stood nearby, their faces hidden in the shadows.

Servants appeared suddenly with large tureens and began setting them down before the people in the courtyard. A frenzy of activity followed. The white cotton tablecloths were flecked with yellow-red turmeric stains as the devotees helped themselves to ladlefuls of the slopping gravy in the tureens. Soon the odor of potato and mutton curry heavily spiced with *garam massala* filled the air. Along with the curry came flat aluminum trays piled high with fluffy, crunchy, oven-cooked naans. Everyone attacked the food with an impatience and zeal that seemed curiously at odds with the spirit of veneration that had been exhibited only moments earlier. Even Master and Bibi, from where Samina sat, were like an ordinary couple entertaining dinner guests. Like all gracious hosts, they were not eating as yet.

Samina could see that Apa Najma did not have an easy undertaking ahead of her. How could she could keep an eye on what Master and Bibi ate or when, and whether Master went to the bathroom, and what he did there, or what he and Bibi did when they were alone? For one thing, the two thugs whose faces were hidden in the shadows, were probably their bodyguards and followed them everywhere.

So, what was she going to do? Samina glanced at Apa Najma and found her staring at Master and Bibi with eyes filled with anger and hatred. She hadn't eaten; the plate before her was empty and clean. Samina knew what she would have done. She would have gone up to the tall, graceful woman with the dangling earrings and said, "Well, Bibi, you should tell my uncle to go home. His wife and children need him." Sitting next to her, close to the black softness of the woolen shawl, Samina would have added, "And Apa Najma must have money to finish medical school, you know." However, Samina was sure that was not at all how Apa Najma might handle the matter. If she had her way, she would yank off the long earrings so Bibi's earlobes would bleed, the blood dripping in tiny blobs to the green silk of her shirt, or she would snatch the *tasbih* from Master's hand and throw it into the gravy in one of the tureens while he watched nonplussed. She might even (depending on how riled she was) push him, making him stagger and fall down.

"Aren't you eating?" Samina asked, shaking her arm.

"No, this isn't food, this is poison," Apa Najma murmured under her breath.

"Be quiet girl, do you want to get in trouble?" Aunt Maman whispered pleadingly.

"We're already in trouble Ammi, can't you see?" Apa Najma retorted, her tone thick with anger. "The poison is already in us."

It was nearly ten when they returned home. Uncle Shah didn't come with them. He put everyone in a *tonga* and handed some money to Kamil, for the fare. Aunt Maman looked the other way when he said he would be late. The *tonga* sprinted from the gates of Master's bungalow with the swiftness of a chariot in a race.

"Go slowly," Aunt Maman admonished the driver, to which the *tongawallah* responded with a chuckle.

"Don't be afraid, it's all right," he said, raising his whip high in the air so that it swished and curled before coming down on the horse's lean shank.

⋅⇒◉⇐⋅

It was Samina's last day at Aunt Maman's. Apa Najma arranged a picnic to the river and they went off with two baskets full of minced meat *parathas*, mango chutney, lime pickles, a potful of potatoes stewed, mashed and sauteed, also sweet, orange carrot *halwa* packed tightly in a brightly flowered china dish, and two thermoses full of tea. A friend of Apa Najma's, Suriya, who lived three houses down from Aunt Maman, was also with them. She was a year or two younger than Apa Najma, about Kamil's age, Samina thought, and was also planning to go to medical college once she passed her Intermediate degree.

Kamil, Rahil and Apa Najma sat in the front seat of the *tonga* with Seema twisting about uncomfortably in Apa's lap, while Suriya, Aunt Maman and Samina sat squeezed together in the back. Holding on to the steel bracket attached to the *tonga's* canopy on her side, a low partition separating the front seat from the back, Samina wished she was sitting behind Kamil. How much she longed to touch him. But it was Suriya who sat upright in that coveted position, her eyes dark with *kajal* as she looked dreamily somewhere in the distance, as if being so close to Kamil was not something she paid any heed to. The *tongawallah*, who was precariously installed on the edge of the right shaft of the *tonga*, his *dhoti* tucked expertly between his legs, his bony back almost touching the wheel, was charging extra because there were so many passengers.

They left the house around nine in the morning, and suffered a bumpy ride for nearly forty-five minutes before arriving at the river. But, bumpy or not, the ride was exhilarating. For one thing, it was mid-December and still quite mild. The sun shone in a cloudless day, there was a breeze that came and went like a whiff of fragrance, and the roads were not cluttered with traffic. Despite the unhappiness the night at the *darbar* had generated, they all felt cheerful this morning, particularly Kamil, who was singing,

> Why do I love you, I cannot tell,
> Why does my heart adore you, I cannot tell . . .

The bells on the horse's harness jingled as if keeping time with the rhythm of Kamil's song. Samina's heart pounded in her breast. She hummed the refrain silently: "I cannot tell, I cannot tell . . ."

There was more singing after their arrival at the river, which was a muddy, meandering rill rather than a river, with a wild growth of reeds bordered by wide patches of algae along its banks. But there were ripples that danced, there was sun gleaming in silver lights on the water. The *parathas* were eaten, and it was on to carrot *halwa* and sipping tea. Kamil asked Samina what she would like to hear.

"What's your favorite song, Samina?"

Samina couldn't believe that he was actually asking her. And he had said her name. Like sonorous notes her own name became music. And he had asked in front of everyone too! She could feel her face getting all hot, slowly like a frying pan. But bravely, courageously, she said,

> This night, this moon, when will it be so again?
> Come and hear the story of my heart.

When Kamil began singing, Samina wished she had the courage to write down her poem on paper and leave it behind for him. Perhaps she could ask Seema to be her messenger, her secret messenger. She would deliver the poem to her brother and then . . . ohhh, how Samina ached with joy, with trepidation that such joy was unreal, that she might lose it before she had grasped it fully.

After the singing came a game of hide-and-seek. Aunt Maman was playing too; she was always ready to join in with every game the children played, even when it was hopscotch or hide-and-seek. Rahil had just been caught, and so it was his turn to stand with his back to everyone and count twenty while the others hid behind bushes and trees. Seema and Samina found themselves huddled together behind some hibiscus and oleander bushes.

"Where's Apa?" Samina asked in a whisper.

"She's with Suriya behind that tree," Seema whispered back pointing to a tree a few feet from them. It was an old oak tree about ten feet wide. The foliage was so dense that the branches nearly touched the ground, creating little pockets of shade where they coiled together in a mesh. Rahil was still counting. Slowly Samina edged toward the tree, which beckoned as a better hiding place. She hadn't gone a few steps when she saw a corner of a deep red *dupatta* that she knew belonged to Suriya jump out surreptitiously like a red rose thrown at a lover. So where's Apa? Samina wondered. Before she went any further she saw Kamil's face next to the *dupatta*, and then Suriya's long, black braid with the colorful, silvery tassels of her *paranda* swinging down her lean, straight back. She stirred. Samina saw Kamil's hand move across her shoulder in a caress. Suriya laughed. A sweet, sugary laugh it was that Samina heard, and then Suriya ran from there, away from Kamil, away from Samina.

They hadn't seen her. Rahil had finished counting and was running in all directions screaming everyone's names. Aunt Maman was the first to be caught. Then came Apa Najma's turn and Suriya's. Kamil had disappeared. Samina was crouching low behind the bushes when Rahil found her, her eyes stinging with hot, scalding tears that she thought were coming from some furnace ablaze behind her eyes. Her heart was clamped with a pain that was different from any pain she had known before, and in her head was a vision of shame. *What did you expect, you chit of a girl*, the vision spoke mockingly, *can't you see she is a woman and you nothing but a scrawny child?*

"Apa Samina, Apa Samina, did you hurt yourself?" Rahil was asking, bending low, peering into her eyes.

The summer after Samina's visit to Sialkot, Aunt Maman left her husband and came to live with her parents in Lahore. She arrived with Rahil and Seema the first week of July, and Kamil came a few days later. Some of Samina's feelings for him deluged her momentarily when he walked in through the front door, especially when she saw his beautiful new mustache, especially when he smiled at her, something she wasn't used to at all. But then she remembered Suriya. Jealousy had made Samina unhappy, wise and cautious, and anyway, the poem she had begun for him had progressed with bitter verses about a broken heart.

In June, before Aunt Maman arrived, news came that Apa Najma had fought with her father. At the *darbar* one evening, she ran into Master's room and called him names. "Blackguard!" she cried, and "Swindler!" Perhaps she had also tried to pull off Bibi's earrings, but the thugs got to her first. The story went that Uncle Shah had to forcibly drag her out, and when he brought her home, he was livid and swore obscenities at his daughter. Apa Najma accused him of being stupid enough to be duped and exploited by a clever con artist. She told him she could take care of her mother and didn't need him, and that she never wanted to see his face again. Samina overheard Aunt Abida tell Amma that Apa Najma pushed her father into a corner when he raised his voice and tried to hit her.

Other pertinent fragments of information floated Samina's way after Aunt Maman had moved in and supplied further notes about Master's fate.

Samina wondered if Uncle Shah would ever come to their house again, listen to music and thump the table with his hands to keep beat with the *tabla*, if Aunt Maman would ever again cook *parathas* in the kitchen in Sialkot or go to Master's *darbar* with her husband. The word 'divorce' quivered in Samina's imagination as a picturesque illusion, its many facets gleaned, like pieces in a kaleidoscope, from all the films she had seen. Would Aunt Maman be forced to hide her face from the world?

One morning, a Sunday, Samina and Sakina were getting ready for the weekly bath. Apa Najma was combing Sakina's hair and looking closely for any lice at the same time; Sakina had been scratching her head more than usual. While waiting to get her mustard oil hair massage, Samina attempted to read a story from *Zebunnisa*, Aunt Abida's favorite magazine (its Urdu still difficult for her). Aunt Abida, meanwhile, had her eyebrows all crinkled up over a piece of embroidery in which a bird with exotic plumage was beginning to emerge among a profusion of brightly colored flowers.

"The *darbar* was in progress," Apa Najma was saying. "Dinner had been served and the disciples were so busy eating no one really noticed Master leave his usual place on the rug on the veranda. A few moments later a boy wandered into Master's toilet while anxiously searching for a place to relieve himself and saw Master sitting on the commode."

"*Hain! Acha?*" Aunt Abida raised a startled face from her bird.

"Yes. The room was filled with a terrible stench, the boy told everyone as soon as he came out and had recovered from the shock of finding Master trying to flush the toilet."

"*Ya* Allah! How awful! So the myth was shattered."

"Yes, finally." Apa Najma rolled her eyes. "The myth was shattered and went down the drain, blocking the toilet. It overflowed!" Apa Najma merrily hit the palms of her hands together in a resounding clap and laughed.

Swiftly, swiftly then, the comb ran through Sakina's hair as Apa Najma's hand flew with the comb. Swoosh! Swoosh!

Never before had Samina heard Apa Najma and Aunt Abida laugh so much, so freely, as if they didn't have a care in the world.

⇢⇒ Largesse ⇐↞

The children were on their way to school. The old man heard their
prattle. There were three of them, the girls Robina and Samar, and the
boy, Ali, just five. He could see them as clearly as if they were standing
near his bed, their lean, gangly bodies clothed in gray flannel uniforms,
their red-and-white satchels, heavy from the weight of books and notebooks, dangling from their small, bony shoulders.

They raced past his door.

"Shhhh! You'll wake up Dadaji," their mother whispered in a cau-
tionary tone. He wished she would let them be. He had been awake
long before the first light slunk in thin white strips through the narrow
slits in the window curtains, and the first pot clanked in the kitchen.
Through the hum in his ears, which had developed during his illness
and would not go away, he had heard snatches of the *azaan* calling to
morning prayer, then the shrill clamorous twittering of sparrows, the
milkman's knock, and finally the metallic clunk-clunk of pots as
Marium started breakfast. And as if that were his cue, he shifted around
in his bed to clear the vibration in his ears; he didn't want to miss the
children's voices.

He deliberately left his bedroom door ajar, unmindful of the cold
night air that stubbornly crept under his bedclothes after midnight and
stiffened his joints. If the children were to find the door open, they
might slip into his room. Once, not too long ago, he had listened,
propped up on his elbows, while they murmured solicitously outside his
room, and he had waited like a man hungering for a morsel of food.
With nervous breath he waited for one slight arm to curl itself around
the door, for one small face to peer at him. But the children were gone
before he could clear his throat and call out to them. The door
remained half-open after that.

"But Abbaji, you'll catch a cold," his daughter-in-law pressed with
some irritation in her voice.

"I need some fresh air, Marium, this room is like a tomb sometimes," he muttered disagreeably, and the children's mother, shaking her head in dismay, left the door open a chink after she brought him a glass of warm milk.

Before his illness he had been an energetic, busy man. A man who liked to stroll on the street where all the shopkeepers knew him well enough to shout *salaams* to him when he went for his walk, where every stone in the pavement was like a block of memory. And he liked to give things. Every afternoon, on his return from his daily walk, he brought home brown milk toffee or crunchy sweets wrapped in multicolored tinsel for the children. Sometimes, he went to the toy shop where the shelves were cluttered with toys and bought dolls with long, silken braids for the girls, and an airplane with tiny, movable wheels for the boy. They waited for him, then, the children, rushing to the door when he knocked with the round, silver orb of his walking stick, crowding at the knob, each child scrambling boisterously to be the first to turn it.

With the stroke came paralysis of his left side, slurred speech so his words sat like stones on his tongue, and worst of all, a clouding of his vision. He was confined to his room after the initial stay at the hospital. At first, as he flowed in and out of uneasy consciousness, he didn't think of the children at all. His mind wandered to the time when he was newly married. His wife, only fourteen, her large round eyes bright and fearful, thought he looked formidable with his dark, bushy mustache and, when he touched her shoulder on his wedding night, she cowered as if he were about to hit her. The old man's dreams were only of his wife now, immediate and real. He forgot he was sick, he even forgot his wife was dead.

One morning, his head cleared a little, he opened his eyes and saw the children standing close to his bed, their faces grave, their eyes apprehensive. They didn't know what to make of him, he knew, they couldn't recognize in the weakened, inert form on the bed any signs of the vitality they had been so familiar with. Where are the sweets, the toys, they wondered perhaps.

They visited him less and less as days dragged into weeks, and preoccupied with childhood concerns and with their own selves, they became strangers to his presence. And so the old man waited, in vain it seemed, for they ran by his door, often played in the veranda across from his room, but did not come in. He heard them giggle, quarrel, scrape the walls as they jostled each other, dash wildly in playing a game of hide-and-seek, and he waited.

It wasn't that he never saw them. Often, when his daughter-in-law settled him into an armchair in the courtyard, bundled in layers of woollen blankets so he could warm himself in the bright unfailing winter sun, the children came up to him and timidly offered salutations. But they didn't stay to talk. When he opened his mouth and attempted to form words laboriously, they gazed at him dumbly and then looked away in awkward silence.

One afternoon, Ali, the boy, seemed to be held back by something on his grandfather's person. It was a watch, an ornate article, now old and tarnished, hanging from a gold chain which had darkened with age. Clipped at one end into the old man's vest, the watch always stayed in his lower vest pocket, taken out only to be wound. The dulled numerals on the yellowed dial were barely discernable. The old man could not remember when he had bought the watch. But he remembered that the orb had once been white and unmarred, the chain shimmering, that once he had timed hours and minutes by its clear dial, managed not just a part of a day, but whole days and nights when he worked as a civil engineer on the Mian Mir canal.

The three children had come up to say "*Salaamalekum* Dadaji." The girls walked away after he smiled and patted their backs. But the boy stayed, his eyes riveted on the chain that hung across his grandfather's chest. For a few moments he watched without moving. Then a tiny finger crawled up hesitatingly, travelling slowly up and down along the chain, the touch so quiet the old man could barely feel it.

"Do you want to see it?" the old man asked, fumbling with the chain, attempting to pull it out with his left hand, his thickly knotted fingers shaky and irresolute. The slippery links eluded his grasp each time as he struggled to pull out the watch. The child watched in silence, his mouth half-open as his grandfather struggled to free the watch from his pocket. He leaned forward expectantly when the watch was finally retrieved from its place of hiding.

The sun shone on its golden surface, making it glitter as if it were a piece of jewelry. The boy gasped. The watch seemed to tick at a brisk tempo, as though propelled by some force which pushed it to go faster, to hasten. The boy wrapped his small, chubby hand over the golden orb and the old man felt a tug at the buttonhole over his heart. He moved toward his grandson.

"Do you know what this is? This is a watch, a very old watch, it is older than you, older than your father."

The boy looked at his grandfather in astonishment. Lifting the watch, he placed it against his right ear and listened intently. His face broke into a smile.

"It's ticking so loudly," he said.

His mother was calling him. Abruptly he let go of the watch, which fell back into the old man's palm with a clinking jangle. While the boy raced to answer his mother's call, slowly and arduously the watch was returned to its place.

For nearly a week the boy didn't ask to see the watch again. But often, while sitting in the veranda, the old man noticed his grandson glancing furtively at it while he was winding it. The old man made a ceremony of winding the watch. Soon after the children had finished lunch and were either playing in the veranda, which remained sunny and warm well into late afternoon, he took out the watch. Squinting, his forehead creased in a frown, his hands thrust into the pockets of his pants, the boy observed his grandfather from a distance. First the old man buffed the watch with his handkerchief, slowly, meticulously, as if this was its first cleaning after years of neglect. Then, holding the orb away from him, he began winding it, painstakingly turning the ridged knob as though it were a musical instrument that he was tuning. The boy tarried until his grandfather had finished winding, had placed the watch next to his ear to listen to its ticking, and finally replaced it into the vest pocket. Then he moved away.

The afternoon excursions into the courtyard were soon suspended; the old man shivered uncontrollably one day and developed a fever. With the electric heater set close to his bed, the quilt made warmer by an additional blanket over it, he slept until the fever slackened its hold. Sweating, he woke up one afternoon to find the children and their mother in his room. She was puttering around as usual, dusting he thought, or maybe cleaning his almirah, tidying up. The children hovered. He saw his grandson playing with the airplane, shouting "Zoom! Zoom!" as his arm rose and fell in swoops, while the two girls whispered amongst themselves, laughing, one of them kicking the chair on which she sat. Before he could form words, his brain fogged again.

But today, he clearly saw the light of day creep into the room through the narrow slits in the window curtain, he heard kitchen pans clanking as Marium supervised breakfast. He waited.

They came. He heard their chatter. He recognized the sound his grandson made when he kicked the wall with his boot as he walked and jumped along the corridor. Their mother scolded him often. "Don't kick the wall, Ali!" But the child was incorrigible. Soon they would leave for school. The old man turned on his side and slipped an unsteady hand under his pillow. The watch, cold and hard, lay nestled in a small depression where it had sunk on account of its weight. He closed his fingers on it and slowly drew it out.

He heard the front door close. Silence followed. The children were gone. He was about to lean back wearily on his pillows when he noticed the door move. At first he thought he had imagined it, a trick of his blurry vision. But a hand was fastened on its rim, then a face appeared from behind it. It was his grandson.

"*Salaamalekum* Dadaji," the boy said, only half of his body in.

"*Walekumsalaam*, son, come in, come in." The old man lifted his weight on his elbows, his breath coming in short, fast spurts. He motioned the boy to enter.

"You will be late for school, where are Robina and Samar?" The ticking of the watch in the palm of his hand made his flesh vibrate.

The boy came forward hesitantly, his hand nervously tapping the rough canvas of his satchel. "They're outside in the garden, the driver is late, Abba is taking us, but he isn't ready yet." His eyes fell on the watch as his grandfather opened his palm.

"Come, sit down, wait here until Abba is ready." The old man patted the edge of the bed, moving back to make room for his grandson.

His bulky satchel dangling awkwardly from his shoulder, the boy sat down and his grandfather quietly handed him the watch. The boy received it silently, chain and watch collapsing heavily in his diminutive palm.

He turned it over and around, he held it to his ear and listened, he thrust it into his shirt pocket and stroked the small bulge over his chest as if he wanted to make sure it was properly placed, he took it out again and felt the rugged edges of the round knob with his finger tips.

The mother was looking for him. Carefully the watch was deposited on the pillow, and smiling broadly, the boy said, "*Khuda hafiz*, Dadaji."

Ali's visits to his grandfather's room grew frequent. He spent more and more of his afternoons after school there, playing with the watch while his grandfather sometimes looked on, sometimes dozed. There was little conversation. To talk was an effort for the old man. Words crowded in his head and on his tongue, but making sounds was tedious and ponderous, like trying to calibrate tiny, integral modules in an electric component with infirm, unsure hands.

Sometimes Ali sprawled on the armchair next to his grandfather's bed, his knees up to his face, and seemed content to merely gaze at the watch, his brows knitted in concentration as he examined the weighty orb at close quarters. But often he hooked the clasp onto the button-hole in his shirt, letting the chain hang in an arc, the watch lodged safely in his pocket. He also enjoyed winding it, the sonorous sound made by the key as he twisted it between his thumb and forefinger, breaking the silence in the room. Always, he returned the watch to his grandfather, and sometimes, on finding him asleep, he would slip it under the pillow himself, pushing it carefully so a slight movement wouldn't bring it tumbling down from the bed to the floor.

Winter was already spent. The days were quite warm, the nights no longer chilly. The window was left open in the old man's room and the door remained ajar as well. His daughter-in-law had taken away the blanket, but the thick quilt remained still. Another two weeks perhaps, before she gave him the weightless, flowered coverlet that his wife had stitched and quilted for him.

"Dadaji, can I take the watch to show Robina and Samar?"

The question surprised him, because Ali rarely engaged him in conversation. His *tasbih* in his hand, the old man had been absently rolling off the beads in prayer. Ali's voice snapped into his drowsiness.

He opened his eyes and saw Ali standing close to him, smiling as he ran a solitary finger over the tarnished, metallic back of the watch, the question burning in his eyes like a flame.

"But, son," the grandfather labored hoarsely, "it is a delicate watch, it can break so easily and it is so heavy. What if you drop it?"

Ali turned the watch over in his hand, his eyes lowered, the smile vanished.

"But I won't drop it, I want to show it to Robina and Samar."

Words, words. The old man felt them like bricks on his tongue. "Bring your sisters here," he said, extending a hand toward his grandson.

"They won't come, they won't come, Dadaji," Ali whimpered, his fingers apprehensively clasping and unclasping the watch.

Was he imagining it, or had the boy moved away from him, to the other side of the room, close to the door? He stretched out an arm and felt the fabric of the boy's shirt under his fingers.

The old man lifted himself. His head swam. "All right, all right, but you will be careful?" He helped Ali place the watch in his pocket.

"I won't break it." A smile spread broadly on Ali's face. "I'll bring it back soon," he said, his face brightening, a hand placed protectively over the pocket where the watch now lay. Ali darted from his grandfather's bedside, kicking the armchair on his way, giving the wall a loud thwack with his hand before he was out of the room.

Through the open doorway, the old man saw that dusk was beginning to crawl into the courtyard beyond. A stillness hung about in the air, broken occasionally by the distant babble of children. Soon it would be dark and all of the courtyard would be plunged into inky darkness.

A Woman of No Consequence

In three weeks I was getting married. Jamila, an old school friend I hadn't seen in nearly seven years, called after she received the wedding invitation.

"Who's the lucky man?" she asked. "Are you in love?"

Her voice stirred memories of childhood I had put away. "His name is Hasan. He's a doctor, and no, I'm not in love, yet." We both laughed. "But tell me, how are you?" I asked.

"I'm all right. We should meet. It's been such a long time since we were together. You're happy?"

"Yes," I said.

She promised to come to lunch. She'd bring her daughter with her, she told me.

Mine was to be a winter wedding. Cool mornings, cloudless, pale skies, bare trees, lots of undiluted sunshine. Everyone could wear brocades, *kemkhabs*, and satins with no sweat and stickiness to worry about. I was lucky I hadn't got stuck with a July wedding like my cousin Zenab, the poor thing. The humidity and heat, compounded by the heavy brocade *dupatta* covering her head made her foundation melt, while the combination of sweat and tears at the moment of farewells completely ruined what was left of the mascara and the eyeliner; imagine looking like a ghoul when you're finally alone with your groom! And the wedding guests looked disgruntled and uncomfortable too, the women hard-pressed in Banarsi saris, gold-embroidered *ghararas*, and elaborately detailed *shalwar-kameez* outfits, the men harried despite the stylish drip-dry summer suits.

Jamila had been married in the summer as well, late June I think, and would have suffered a fate similar to Zenab's except that she had the foresight to use only a very thin layer of foundation and rouge. With her characteristically mischievous smile she informed us of how she would re-apply her makeup after the crying and goodbyes.

In the days when the only eye makeup was a thin line of *kajal*, it didn't really matter how much you wept. Also, the *dupatta*, pulled all the way down to chin level, hid your face so whatever smears or leaks there were, no one was privy to. Now, of course, times have changed. We know we will cry; it is in the nature of wedding farewells that brides will shed tears of sorrow at the thought of leaving the security and certitude of life in the home of their parents. But the *dupatta* no longer conceals the face for us educated types. The trick then, lies in cleverly safeguarding makeup. Jamila was an expert at clever tricks.

Who could forget the story of spitting in the holy water at the church at St. Mary's, or the incident of the gum—six sticks in all—chewed to a clayey, gray mass, surreptitiously, and rather skillfully affixed to Mother Loyola's habit one afternoon in the summer of tenth standard? Jamila had been a free spirit. We, the more timorous ones who quaked in our boots when confronted with the wrath of the nuns, envied her. She was undaunted by authority, receiving raps on her knuckles for misdemeanors with a grin broadly mapped across her small, angular face. She never winced, never indicated by word or action that the punishment hurt and that didn't make Mother Loyola happy; Mother Loyola disapproved of girls who smiled courageously when they were being punished.

When I opened the door for Jamila I couldn't conceal my amazement, I could do nothing about the way my eyes flew open. I simply stared.

"*Assalaamalekum!*" She ran toward me and we hugged. Her daughter, no older than two, frail, her eyes distrustful as some children's are when they are among strangers, clutched a corner of her mother's *kameez* and hid her face from me.

Who was this woman? Was this Jamila, Jamee, as we had called her at St. Mary's, the ever-impish, ever-mirthful Jamee? She was pregnant. The skin on her face was papery and ashen, the lines around her mouth had hardened, dark shadows began at the edges of her eyes and extended to her cheeks like permanent skin discolorations, the eyes yellow and lifeless. Her hair, which I remembered as shiny and bouncy with curly tendrils, was straggly and streaked untidily with gray. But she was as old as I! It was a face and a body that seemed to have been ravaged. By time, by marriage, by children? My God, what had happened?

We talked. Of this and that at first. Awkwardly we steered clear of the question that she undoubtedly saw in my eyes. Secretly I cursed myself for being so obvious. I stroked her little girl's cheek, made faces at her and then watched in embarrassment as the child drew back from me.

"Don't mind her, Zohra, she's very shy."

"She's so cute. Your first?"

"No, my third. My oldest daughter is four, Zeba is three, and Safia here has just turned two."

We began reminiscing about St. Mary's. She told me she had registered her daughters there.

"You won't believe this, but Mother Loyola is still around, bent out of shape and all, and so fat you'd wonder how she can walk. Actually she waddles." Jamila giggled, covering her mouth the way she used to so the nuns wouldn't catch her giggling and punish her for being giddy.

I couldn't imagine Mother Loyola waddling. She was tall and the most athletic of the nuns at school. When she tossed the ball into the basket she jumped almost three feet into the air. Or so it seemed to us then.

We had lunch. Over tea I asked Jamila why she wasn't teaching any more.

"It was just too much, with the girls and taking care of the house." She avoided my gaze. Then her lips opened in a tired smile. "Children are a handful, you know."

"And how have you been all this time?" I couldn't help myself. The question slipped out.

"You're getting married, Zohra, you don't want to hear my story. It's just one of those crazy things, kismet and all, you know."

The story was long and tortuous. Jamila had been right. It wasn't the sort of thing you needed to hear two weeks before you were getting married. But there never really is a right or wrong time for such stories. If you don't hear them, don't tell them, they fester like uncared for wounds and become pus-ridden, gangrenous, untreatable.

The scenario was age-old. Only Jamee was the innovation. She was naive. She thought the world was St. Mary's. When her mother-in-law expressed disappointment after the birth of her first child, a girl, Jamee was hurt. Her husband, Kamal, consoled her. "Mothers are like that, they always want grandsons," he told her. The child was named Saba, Persian for easterly morning breeze, sweets were distributed to family members and friends, and in a few days the scowl left her mother-in-law's face.

"But I too wanted a son, not for my mother-in-law, for myself, for Kamal. We decided we shouldn't wait."

Her daughter had fallen asleep on the settee. Jamee stroked her absently, smoothing her frock, patting down her short baby curls.

"My second baby was another daughter. This time my mother-in-law started grumbling, muttering under her breath whenever she held the baby in her lap, saying things like, 'Where are the dowries going to come from? Who will carry Kamal's name? Without a son a man is finished.' It all sounds very melodramatic and sappy, but believe me, something happened to her."

"But what about Kamal?" If he loved her, why didn't he protect her? I thought possessively.

"Well, she didn't say anything in front of him. But behind his back she made sarcastic remarks whenever she had the chance. She began insinuating I would never have a son, that I was doomed to having only daughters."

"And you ignored the stupid woman, didn't you?" I edged forward in my seat, anxious to hear that Jamee didn't give in to the old crone.

"No, Zohra, how can you ignore a person who's living in the same house as you are? In a strange way I began to think she was right. I felt something was wrong with me. Anyway, I got pregnant again when my second one was barely five months old. I miscarried in my third month and my mother-in-law wouldn't let me hear the end of it. She used harsh words and taunted me. I used to wonder if it was widowhood that had hardened her. My mistrust of her kept growing."

Jamee straightened her shoulders and lifted her chin. "You're not going to believe this, but I decided to show her. I was pregnant again within three months of my miscarriage. And guess what? I had another daughter, Safia, this sweet thing here, who won't let me out of her sight for one minute. I could see that Kamal was beginning to be affected by his mother's attitude, not visibly, not consciously perhaps, but he's her son, after all." Breathless, Jamee leaned wearily against the cushions on the settee.

I got up and poured her a glass of orange juice. She took the glass from me silently and slowly sipped the juice.

"But didn't you discuss the situation with someone in your family? What about your mother, your sister? You're not alone in the world."

"I talked to my mother often, and my sister as well, but she just kept getting angrier and angrier at Kamal and my mother-in-law. She even told me I had become a child-bearing machine, that I wasn't a real woman anymore. We fought bitterly, and that was all. You see I knew she was right, but I felt helpless. I had to have a son or it was all over for me." With a protective hand on her swollen belly, Jamee changed her position, nervously twisting her hair before continuing.

"I will be a woman of no consequence until I produce a son. So I kept trying. My husband encouraged me, my mother-in-law prodded and pushed. I became pregnant again when Safia was six months old." Her eyes filled. Safia was stirring. Jamee rubbed a hand over her cheeks and bent over the sleeping child. "Shhh . . ." she crooned softly.

"I should be happy," she said, turning to me after Safia was still again. "But something inside me keeps collapsing, like there was a wall somewhere and it's slowly crumbling and taking me aground with it. I find myself incapable of expressing love or affection. Kamal keeps to himself a lot, he's busy at work, he's an accountant for a firm and he comes home late most days. I've lost interest in clothes, in my appearance. Sometimes two whole days go by before I have a thought to combing my hair properly. At night I can't sleep because I'm tormented by the thought that if I have another daughter my mother-in-law will make Kamal remarry . . . " She looked at and raised a hand. "I know, it's a stupid idea, an idea fit for an illiterate woman, but Zohra, there are men out there, and you know it, who are remarrying for sons, for children, for God knows what else."

"But if he loves you, and I'm sure he does . . ."

"Are you? How can you be sure? I'm not. I don't trust him, I don't trust his mother."

"But has he said anything? Maybe you're imagining this, Jamee."

"I hope I am, I hope this is only in my head, but unless I know, really know, is there any way out for me?"

"Of course there is. You're a talented, intelligent woman. You know it doesn't matter whether your children are all boys or all girls, and if you confide in your husband he'll tell you the same thing, I'm sure." My words had a tinny ring to them, as if they were echoes, not real sounds. I had no experience of husbands or mothers-in-law. How could I say any of this with authority?

"I've confided in him," Jamee said, pulling at her hair again. "I told him what I was going through. He said the usual things: 'Ignore Amma, take care of yourself, I would like a son, but it won't be the end of the world if we have another girl,' etc., etc. He's been too busy to really listen to what I have to say. Too busy to put his arms around me and comfort me. Do you know how long it's been since he put his arms around me? Three years. We make love at night, he rolls over and snores in five minutes and that's that. Do you remember how we used to imagine we'd always be romantic, even when we were eighty years old, and that we'd write passionate love letters to our husbands when we were away from each other?"

It was a pact made when we were in tenth standard and had just seen *An Affair to Remember.* Jamee, Zenab, another friend, Samina and I, we all got together at Jamee's house on the pretext that we were going to study for an exam. Since Jamee's parents were away in Multan, and only her older sister, who was friendly and lenient, was around, our journey to Plaza Cinema and the afternoon with Cary Grant and Deborah Kerr were unmarred by snarls of one sort or another.

"Let's make a pact," Jamee said suddenly during the *tonga* ride home. The film had left us quiet and contemplative; we had all shed tears in the dark, we knew. "Let's promise we'll always be romantic," she continued excitedly, "even when we've had our menopause and lost some teeth and our hair's all gray."

We giggled at first in response to her startling suggestion.

"Oh, please, Jamee, I don't want to think about gray hair and menopause," Zenab protested. "And anyway, where are we all going to find our Cary Grants?"

"We'll find them. Come on, let's make a pact then." Jamee bristled with undisguised energy. "Let's call it the Treaty of the Lovelorn and refer to it as TL for short."

"And if one of us fails to comply with its terms, will there be punishment?" Samina raised an eyebrow inquiringly.

Jamee was quick to retort. "Of course. What's a pact without compliance?"

What a long time ago that was. Or seemed. "Yes, I remember the pact. We also decided we would hold hands in public, and not care what anyone thought."

"How silly we were, Zohra, how foolish." Jamila plucked at the *dupatta* on her shoulders. Tears gathered in her eyes again, her face broke up, crumpled, and she covered her face with her hands. "You're wondering if I haven't gone mad, if I'm not quite insane, aren't you?" she said, without caring any more to wipe the tears that ran down her face.

"No, no, oh God, Jamee, of course not. I just feel so helpless. I hope you have a son this time, but my dear, there's no guarantee."

"I know. But I have to try. It's like nothing else is important anymore, not even any of my girls or my mother or father, anyone."

Safia was awake. She squirmed and pouted. Jamee took her in her lap and tidied her hair. "Do you think I'm crazy?" she asked me.

"No. But why didn't you ever call, write? Maybe if we had kept in touch . . ." Why hadn't I called?

"We weren't in Lahore. Kamal was posted to Karachi where we stayed for many years. Actually I just didn't feel like seeing anyone. I felt like a recluse, like someone who had something to hide. Anyway, I'm due in three weeks, so I won't be able to make it to your wedding, I don't think. I'm leaving for Karachi tomorrow and you'll be leaving for the U.S. in a month. I'll be with my mother. Don't forget to write."

I promised I would write. She assured me she would take care of herself. We hugged, I kissed her little girl's pallid cheeks, and mother and daughter left. The winter day had sunk into dark twilight, hastily as winter days are wont to do in Lahore, a chill had crept up in the air and a breeze slunk about with a restless, shuffling sound.

--=◎=--

The pain in her right leg drew along the side of her body in one searing motion and she gasped. Then, before she had a chance to recover from the shock of the pain that racked her, a slow, dull heaviness gathered at the small of her back and began growing in tight, short spurts. She sat up quickly and clasped her swollen abdomen with both hands. Within minutes the sensation, stronger and sharper this time, returned. So this was it. Her heart moved in her chest as if there was nothing there to hold it down. Her mouth was filled with the taste of dust. The heaviness became pain, waves, layered, one upon another, thick. A whirlwind, a storm.

She climbed out of bed slowly, one hand still tightly held against her belly as though she was afraid if she let go she'd lose what she was holding inside. Slipping her feet into the slippers that lay beside the bed, she moved swiftly toward the bedroom door. Bent over with the force of pain she clambered through the cold night air of the veranda and entered her mother's room.

"Amma, Amma, wake up, the pains have started, Amma, Amma," she whispered hoarsely, bending over her mother's sleeping form, violently shaking her shoulder.

⊷≈◉〓⊷

She wavered in and out of consciousness. She felt as if a great big stone which had been fastened to her womb was being ripped away, forced asunder from where it was joined to her flesh. Sometimes she opened her eyes and saw blinding light, when she heard voices that seemed to come to her like whispers, conspiratorial whispers, secretive, enigmatic. Then she felt nothing. In her head another voice wove itself over other noises, a voice that kept saying, like the lilting refrain of a song, "Let it be a boy, dear God, let it be a boy, let it be a boy . . ."

After what seemed to her like endless waiting, someone spoke to her, but she couldn't decipher the words. She muttered her prayer again and found that her lips were stiff, incapable of movement. There was a face bending over hers. Through the mist in her eyes she saw it was her mother. What was her mother doing in the delivery room?

Suddenly she felt that a flood had been let loose from within her, warm and gushing like a river opened at the dam. Then something was wrenched from her, a part of her flesh, she thought. She screamed until she felt she could no longer breathe. I'm dying, she said to herself, I'm dying and who will care for my children?

Coming out of a haze she clamored, "What is it? Is it a boy? Is it a boy?" She pleaded, but no one seemed to pay attention to what she was saying. Before long she drifted into slumber.

When she opened her eyes again she found herself in a strange room. Bare, with white walls, a small window on which dull-colored curtains limply hung against the morning light. The recovery room, she thought. She looked about her frantically and saw the bundle on a table at the far end of the room.

Lifting herself on her elbow, she raised her body and tried to get into a sitting position. Her head swam, a stabbing pain surged along the insides of her thighs and her belly contracted, convulsed achingly. She slowly swung her legs over the side of the bed, feeling a warm trickle between her legs as she did so.

Carefully wrapping the white hospital sheet around her waist, she got off the bed and shuffled over to the table. The baby had been wrapped in a woolen shawl she had knitted for Saba, a blue and white design. She lifted a corner of the shawl. The baby was asleep, its eyes tightly shut. Why had they covered its face?

"It's a boy," she whispered, her eyes filling with hot, scalding tears.

"Oh God, it's a boy!" Leaning against the table so she wouldn't lose her balance, she gingerly lifted the baby from the table.

"My son . . ." She uttered the words joyfully, repeating them over and over again. But why is he so still? she wondered. Her breasts pulsated, burned, ached. She clasped the baby to her and returned to her bed. Sitting down, she pulled up her hospital gown and bared her engorged breast.

"Come on, come on, here, here," she cooed softly as she tried to force the nipple into the baby's small, quiet mouth.

⋆⋅═◉⊂═⋅⋆

The Connecticut snow, sneaking up on us again this year while we still had leaves on the ground, was accumulating in soft, white mounds. I was pregnant with my third child. The unborn baby had been given a name—Zenab—in the hope that it was going to be a girl. A daughter after two sons, a friend for my old age, I explained philosophically to Dr. Happel, my obstetrician, when she gave me that sidelong look accompanied by a smirk that said, silently, "Yes, sure, anything you say." When, in the last stages of labor, spurred by Dr. Happel as if this were a sack race and not the occasion of giving birth, feeling as if life itself were ebbing from me, I clutched and unclutched my sweaty palms, I said to God, "Let it be a girl, dear God, let it be a girl!"

Of course, God couldn't do much at this point, and it was another boy. The nurses, Betty and Lizabeth, who had been with me throughout the six hours of labor and delivery, made light of my disappointment and said, "Try again, Zohra."

For a whole day after the baby and I came home, the two older brothers continued to call him 'Zenab.' We finally named him Kasim Ali and Doctor Happel said, "Maybe you'll have a daughter-in-law who'll be a friend in your old age." And one day, as I changed the bloodied little cotton swab on his circumcised penis, I remembered Jamila. I felt guilty. As if I had taken something that didn't belong to me, as if I had cheated on an exam.

But I wanted a friend for my old age, I said to my absent friend. We've both lost something.

⊸⊸ A Matter of Togetherness ⊷⊷

Cecilia Shabir, whose husband was Raza Shabir, the famous trial lawyer, never converted to Islam. What some of her husband's relatives, friends and acquaintances must have said! Arifa could hear their voices, clear, unequivocal. And she could see their faces; such disappointment, such heartache written on every contortion, on every face.

"What a shame, he has no control over her," "What will they do about the children?" "*Uff!* There will be such problems," or, simply, "*Hai, hai,* such bad luck."

After all, in those days conversion was a common enough occurrence. Coming up against unrelenting mothers-in-law (who, finding their authority threatened, would throw violent tantrums, feign illness, and all else failing, sulk), and a wall of other equally stubborn family members, a non-Muslim bride had no recourse but to convert. A change of name at least was warranted: Fatima, Zenab, Amina, Maryam for the traditional ambience, or Anjum, Parveen, Saba, or Nuzhat if you wanted to be current and faddish. However, Cecilia, an Anglo-Indian who probably knew a great deal about such mothers-in-law, obviously prevailed over the opposition she faced (at what cost, she never did tell any of her colleagues at St. Mary's), and kept her name as well as her religion.

She was already something of a legend, a grand old lady of English literature, when Arifa joined the staff of St. Mary's as a high-school Urdu teacher in the eighties. It was rumored that she knew all of *Twelfth Night, Hamlet,* and *Othello* by heart. But looking at her, watching her go about her work in that quiet, diffident manner of hers, listening to her as she bent her head to one side solicitously and delivered remarks in a sing-song manner, one found it difficult to believe any of the stories told about her unwavering attachment to literature and her passionate obsession with goading her girls to get A's in their Senior Cambridge exam.

Rotund, yet not really fat, she was of medium height and was never seen in anything but a sari, a dress she seemed to handle with perfect ease. The front gathers were always neatly in place like the folds of an unfurled fan, the *pallu* always resting solidly on her left shoulder, never slipping. On her face she carried a somber, rather pensive expression, a kind of worried look which owed much, Arifa thought, to her thickly creased forehead. The most prominent feature of her physiognomy was her smile. When her small lips stretched in a brief expression of amusement, a shadow seemed to lift, revealing the face of a young girl, happy, almost bashful.

Even as she and Arifa discussed the ingredients of *karahi gosht*, she looked earnest and thoughtful, as if the question at hand was not how much yogurt was to be used with one pound of lamb, but rather a soliloquy from *Hamlet*: should one explain the text with reference to the context or paraphrase it? Since Arifa didn't know much about Shakespeare, or English literature for that matter, Arifa was sure they were drawn together because of her enthusiasm for new recipes and her own attempts to take cooking beyond the mundane. They forgot the difference in their ages when they embarked on lively and animated discussions about recipes.

Desserts were her favorite subjects, and it was during the enumeration of ingredients for *shahi tukre* that she surprised Arifa with a question which made her realize how little she knew about her.

"Arifa," she began, her thick, brief eyebrows lifted and joined in arcs above her eyes, "I want your advice about something."

She seemed agitated; her face became flushed and she moved restlessly on the edge of her seat as though struggling with a bit of wayward air.

"Yes, what is it, Mrs. Shabir?" Obviously this was not about the ratio of milk to sugar.

"Tell me," she continued, "do you think my husband and I can be buried in the same cemetery?" She suddenly looked mournful.

Having come upon the heels of "Won't cream be better than milk?" the question caught Arifa off guard.

One doesn't often dwell too much on how one is to fare in death without just cause (illness and the like), and Arifa, being only in her late forties, had not had any reason to ponder over such somber subjects with regard to herself. Also, where one is buried is something taken quite for granted. For example, Arifa knew she'd have a place in the cemetery in Mian Mir where her parents were resting, also her grand-parents and her uncles. Unless, of course, death came when she wasn't in Pakistan. Who knows, it might catch up with her during her travels to Europe with her husband, who was very fond of traveling. The thought wasn't a happy one; Arifa shrugged it aside hurriedly.

Anyway, Cecilia Shabir didn't look ill. She hadn't missed school once in the year and a half Arifa had been at St. Mary's, and except for the usual winter sniffles and coughing bouts during the flu season, Arifa didn't recall ever seeing her seriously indisposed.

"Mrs. Shabir, what a thing to say." Arifa smiled, hoping to shake her out of this melancholy mood. Ignoring her smile, Cecilia Shabir continued to frown sadly.

They were alone in the teachers' lounge where they had been cor-recting notebooks before drifting off into a discussion about *shahi tukre*. Second period was into its third quarter. Anne Blythe, who taught math and happened to share this free period with them, had stepped out into the hallway to talk to a student, and except for the distant strains of a military march being played in the gym in the adjoining building and the muted sounds of teachers addressing students in quiet, even-paced tones, a lulling silence typical of late Lahore spring afternoons hung about the school building.

Cecilia leaned forward in her seat; a chubby-fingered hand solemn-ly raised in response to Arifa's remark. Suddenly Arifa felt as if she were her student, as if she had to listen attentively while Mrs. Shabir expressed an opinion. She swallowed her smile.

"Arifa, this is something I have been thinking about a great deal lately. One has to, you know, think about the end, that is." She absently brushed a hand over the *pallu* of her sari, then adjusted the folds that fell still and measured over her knees. Her lips were pursed thoughtful-ly.

"But Mrs. Shabir . . ."

She cut Arifa short with the wave of her hand. "I'm not so young any more, you know. In another year I'll be retiring. Isn't this the right time to make such arrangements?"

"Well," Arifa ventured nervously since the jump from recipes to death had been too precipitous. She wasn't sure how to respond. This was just as difficult as Shakespeare. Arifa took a deep breath. "As far as I know, there's no provision for a Christian burial at a Muslim cemetery. But you should check with an expert."

"That's why I'm asking you, Arifa. I don't want to talk about this with my husband, you know, he'll just get upset, and there's no one else I can take into my confidence. You can find out for me, can't you?"

Cecilia's anxiety at being separated from her husband in death was understandable. But was there a way out for her? Secretly Arifa was convinced there was none. Cemeteries are notoriously insular places. There are both Sunni and Shia cemeteries for Muslims who wish to maintain the purity of faith even in death. But a Christian may not have a Christian burial in a Sunni, Shia or other type of Muslim place of rest. Her concern was indeed legitimate. Arifa fussed with the crochet edging on her *dupatta*. And she was no expert. Cecilia Shabir continued without waiting for her answer.

"I asked Father James and he said it wouldn't be possible to give Raza Muslim rites, you know *namaz*, etc., so he can't have a place in our cemetery. That's why I decided to ask you."

But will she have a place in his? Arifa wondered uneasily. Not if she wished Christian rites. Oh God, what a mess this was.

"I'll check with the *maulavi sahib* who teaches my son the Koran. Give me a day or two." Arifa patted Cecilia Shabir's pudgy hand.

Arifa's promise appeared to put Cecilia's mind at ease. She immediately looked relaxed. But without the slightest bit of change in her tone, she asked, "Now about the cream," just as Anne Blythe returned from her conference with the student. Relieved, Arifa quickly flung herself into cream and sugar ratios.

The topic of cemeteries didn't come up again simply because Arifa didn't get a chance to talk to *maulavi sahib*. He came to the house every evening, but when he finished the lesson, he was always in a hurry to leave; slurping over his teacup he munched quickly on the biscuits Arifa sent him while her son was still reviewing the last line of his lesson and when Arifa went after him he was already on the driveway, his white *shalwar* flapping as he rode his clinking cycle away from the house. Finally one day Arifa's son had fever, the lessons had to be cancelled and Arifa stalled *maulavi sahib* with tea, sugar biscuits and potato *pakoras*. This was her chance to get the information she needed. She mentioned the subject casually without going into any specific details.

"No, no, daughter," he said ominously, shaking his head and stroking his long, dappled beard at the same time. "There is no question of having any other kind of burial except a Muslim one. Yes, if the person converts just before death, then that is another matter, just the recitation of the *kalima* in good faith will do."

What was Arifa to tell Cecilia? She felt guilty, as if the cemetery were her personal property and she was deliberately keeping her out. Convert to Islam, was she to advise her colleague, or stay out? You may have forced yourself in your husband's world in life, but in death you cannot be with him. You're an outsider. Arifa couldn't bring herself to broach the subject with her. Fortunately they were rarely alone, and Cecilia didn't give her any hint that she was eagerly waiting for an answer, except once, but just as she had lifted a finger in query, Anne Blythe burst in noisily with the news that Mother Dominic, everyone's favorite nun, was leaving Lahore.

In the weeks that followed, Arifa and Cecilia Shabir continued to examine recipes. Emily Clark, a younger English teacher, was getting married. So there was also talk of wedding dresses, the service that was to be held at St. Joseph's, the reception afterward at Burt Institute. In all of this Cecilia offered to give Emily her lace handkerchief for something old. Arifa didn't understand at first, but then Cecilia explained, with that rare twinkle in her eye and her bashful smile illuminating her deeply lined face. What a quaint custom, Arifa thought, remembering how she was planning to give her emerald *kundan* necklace to her oldest son's wife when he got married, but was afraid her daughter-in-law (whoever she might be), might not like it and exchange it for something else later, and Arifa was too fond of her *kundan*.

One afternoon, during recess, while Emily was showing Anne Blythe some swatches, Cecilia, who had been sipping tea from her thermos cup, suddenly fell forward in her chair. Arifa had just finished correcting her last notebook when she saw her keel over. All of them ran to her. The tea from her cup had spilled in dark, muddy streaks over her crisp, white cotton sari. Anne and Arifa helped her straighten up while Emily ran to fetch Anne's husband, Dr. Blythe, the hygiene teacher and also the school physician.

Cecilia's face was nearly the color of her sari and she was breathing laboriously. Oh God, she's having a heart attack, Arifa thought wildly, her mind crowded with other, grimmer images as well.

"Are you all right, Mrs. Shabir?" Arifa asked gently, bending over her with a glass of iced water.

She remained a little breathless, but some of her color returned. She didn't seem to be in pain.

"I'm fine, I just felt a little weak, that's all. Don't worry girls, and could someone ring my husband please?"

Dr. Blythe arrived promptly, took her pulse and pronounced her well. "Just a bit of dizziness," he said in his good-humored manner.

That was the last time any of them saw Cecilia in school. She was taking a much-needed rest, Mother Rosario, the principal, solemnly informed everyone. Three weeks later Cecilia suffered a heart attack. Anne Blythe tearfully transmitted the news. Arifa's heart sank; she wished she had not been so reticent with the truth. At assembly that morning Mother Rosario led the school in a short prayer for Mrs. Shabir's good health.

Arifa went to see her at the Lahore United Christian Hospital. She was still in ICU so Arifa could only stay five minutes.

She murmured a faint hello when Arifa touched her hand, covering it with her own.

"How are you?" Arifa asked, leaning toward Cecilia's wasted, wan face. She was obviously not well at all. Her skin was ashen and her eyes looked blue and watery.

"Better," she whispered hoarsely.

The skin on her face had sagged, as if dragged down by an invisible force and the furrows on her brow were flat. The look of perpetual anxiety had disappeared. Instead, she looked calm, untroubled, her lips no longer pursed in consternation. Under the bluish-white hospital bedsheet, her body seemed like a child's, lean, narrow, still, as in sleep.

At the side of her bed, on a white, featureless table was a blue plastic water pitcher, a glass covered with a netted doily, a tiny box of Kleenex, and a rosary. The beads were smaller than one would find in a *tasbih*, but if one didn't see the gold crucifix, it would be hard to say at first glance that it wasn't a beautifully crafted *tasbih*.

When Arifa visited Cecilia again, it wasn't at the hospital. It was at her home. She was laid out on the veranda of her Davis Road house on a Muslim bier, in readiness for her journey to her husband's cemetery.

Betrayed in death? By whom? Was this a ploy her husband had come up with to keep her by his side? In one sense she was going to get her wish, but not quite as she had envisioned it.

Her body, draped in a crisp white cotton *kaffan*, rested on a wooden *charpai*. Garlands of roses, which had begun to wilt and curl at the edges were arranged in rows over the shroud, especially around her face. A woman who dies before her husband is lucky, they say, so she must have flowers, red flowers, on her bier, a bride she still is in death.

Her face, whatever little was visible in the midst of the red halo of roses, was the face of an old, sad woman. Above her head was a strip of green cloth on which the *kalima* was etched in gold letters: *There is no God but Allah and Muhammad is His prophet.*

⟶ A Man of Integrity ⟵

The letter came in an ordinary white envelope, the kind one can buy fifty of for ten rupees. Somewhat transparent, crumpled because it was thin and flimsy, it was obviously not an official envelope, which was why he looked at it anxiously. Why was a personal letter posted to his office address? Was it bad news?

He tore open the envelope and removed the piece of paper that, unlike the envelope, was more expensive looking, heavy, unlined, with a watermark—special writing paper. The ink was Mont Blanc blue, the writing, in English, neat and ordered. He began reading:

> Dear Sami *Sahib*:
> You will be surprised no doubt when you get this letter. You will wonder who is writing to you at the office, why the hand-writing doesn't look familiar, if it's a personal letter, etc., etc. The letter itself is harmless, I will say right away, so don't worry unnecessarily. And it's from a stranger. You don't know me. We have never met. Perhaps we have seen each other, as people walking in the streets see each other, but we have never met. Although a meeting may have taken place, the sort that takes place at a crowded party where people who don't know each other are randomly introduced. Anyway, this is all conjecture. The fact is I know you quite well, but you know nothing about me.

Sami quickly turned over the letter to see who had signed it. Nadira. A woman. He knew no one of that name. His heart began thumping against his ribs and he felt sweat gather on his forehead like prickly heat. Surely this meant trouble. These were turbulent times. People were often singled out for no obvious reason and made to suffer in the most humiliating ways. He had an enemy. Someone who wished to degrade him. And this was a common ploy. A woman appears from nowhere and places at his door an accusation, says for example that she is with child, that the child is his. Just recently poor Kamil Khan, the famous cricketer and now politician, had suffered such a fate. But he, Sami Ahmed, M.B.B.S, general practitioner, was neither famous nor a politician. Why him? Brushing a hand across his brow, he flipped over the sheet and resumed reading.

For a strange woman to be writing to a man, especially one who is married, is beyond the bounds of good behavior, I agree, but I have written to you after much thought. This is not the act of a thoughtless, insensitive woman. For a whole year I have wondered what to do. Can I be candid? You seem like a lonely man. You stay long hours in your clinic, even when you have no patients. Why do you not go home to your wife, your two children? I do not wish to be rude, but I think you are running from them. Perhaps you need a friend. Perhaps I can be your friend. Is it possible that we meet somewhere?

There was no mention of a child. As yet. The paper in Sami's hands shook and his breath came fast, as if he had been running. Nevertheless, this had all the signs of a conspiracy to dishonor him. Doctors were common targets for such scandal. It was a patient. A woman who had been coming to him for some time and now had seen her chance for extortion. Would she want only money? The letter had ended. The last sentence said, "I will write again," and she had signed it, simply, "Nadira."

"Doctor *saab*, shall I send in the next patient?" Sami's attendant, Rafi, a young man given to illusions of superiority because he worked in a doctor's office, showed his head through the door.

"No, no, wait a few minutes." Sami dismissed him with a wave of his hand. He wanted to concentrate. Who was this woman, this . . . this Nadira? He had seen innumerable women in the last six years of practice. Which one was she? His mind refused to work. Other, unrelated images pushed for his attention. Again and again he saw pictures of the young girl for whom he had harbored a pubescent passion when he was fifteen. A long-necked, sprightly girl, she was seventeen, perhaps, or eighteen, and came to hang up her family's wash on the roof of the house next door. Bending, lifting up her arms, reaching up on her toes, turning, stretching her lithe body, she strung the clothes on the line with the grace and energy of a dancer. Bewitched the first time he saw her, the kite he had been flying forgotten, Sami watched her in a daze, the string in his hand suddenly loose, the kite swelling away from him, tugging at his hand as it rose and plunged, his mouth dry, his groin burning with desire.

"Doctor *saab*, it's Mrs. Niazi, she says she's in a rush." The thickly mustached face of his attendant appeared behind the door again.

"*Acha, acha*, send her in. How many more do we have?"

"Just two, Doctor *saab*, the old *mai* with a stomach ache and Bashir, Kamal *saab*'s gardener. He has fever today and he can barely move, his whole body is aching he says and I told him he will need Disprin . . . "

"*Acha*, go now," Sami said impatiently. Rafi sometimes fancied himself a nurse.

Mrs. Niazi was, like Sami, in her late thirties. As with so many of her counterparts, she had little to do, far too much to eat, and subsequently had put on weight. Now she was complaining of shortness of breath along with her frequent headaches. She was convinced she had high blood pressure and suspected that Sami deliberately withheld the information from her. Her large black shawl hanging carelessly from her shoulders and nearly trailing the floor as was the custom, she walked in and greeted Sami in the manner patients greet their family doctors, as if they are uncles, brothers, or at least old friends. Sami looked at her closely. She was stout, her face was puffy, there were dark bluish circles under her eyes, and her hair, cut short, was pinned away from her face, revealing gray streaks at the hairline. How beautiful she must have been once, when the eyes were bright, the skin taut and smooth, the body and spirit untarnished by neglect and apathy. She deposited herself in the chair across from his desk with a sigh, crossed her legs and shook her head despondently.

"Doctor *saab*, you have to give me something for my headaches," she said, pressing down on her forehead with one heavily ringed, plump hand. "Like this I'll die."

No, it could not be her. She depended too much on him. It was someone who had no fear in her heart, who was daring and presumptuous. Who then? The image of the girl from his youth rose up in his mind again. Why, after all these years, did he have to think of her? It wasn't a memory he was very proud of. He had behaved foolishly. He wouldn't want his own son to be so enamored.

He had written a letter to her, calling her 'queen of my dreams,' because he did not know her name, secured the letter to a jewelled plastic comb with a rubber band and had then thrown his gift and the letter over the parapet when she was pulling down laundry one afternoon. She knew she had an admirer on the rooftop across from hers and she had smiled enchantingly at him more than once. But the letter, a fervid, incoherent admission of his passion, fell into the wrong hands. Just as she stooped to pick up his epistle, her fingers still clutching a white sheet that she had partly dislodged from the line, an older woman, probably an aunt or her mother, appeared as if from nowhere from behind the white billowing bedsheet that flapped noisily in the wind, and grabbed the comb along with the letter still attached to it.

Sami knew that the disaster he had courted for so long had finally arrived at his door. A complaint was lodged with his mother, who, in turn, warned his father, who then boxed his ears and threatened to break his legs if he went up to the rooftop again. Love had clutched at his heart many times in later years, but none of his other attachments had generated the excitement this one had.

"No, no, Mrs. Niazi, you won't die, we won't let you," Sami said, smiling benevolently at his patient. "Now what seems to be the trouble?"

That afternoon, driving home in his red Suzuki that needed tuning and stalled and coughed frequently, he continued to think of the letter, which was now snug in his left pocket. Zaheen, his wife, should be warned, he decided. She should be told about the letter and the danger it carried. There was no reason to conceal it from her. He was not a man of secrets and there wasn't much in his life his wife or any one in his family didn't know about. After all, his was an uneventful life. Every morning, after a ritual of bathing and shaving, reading the paper and eating a breakfast that was always the same, he left for his clinic, saw patients until one, then came home for lunch and a long nap, returned to the clinic at five, saw more patients, read for an hour from the medical journals from America he subscribed to faithfully, and left for home around ten. If the Lahore traffic, which was particularly murderous at that time, didn't slow him down too much he made it back to his home in Shadman around ten-thirty. Zaheen didn't seem to mind that he came home so late so he wasn't worried if the traffic delayed him further. On Fridays he took the evening off and that was when he took Zaheen and the two boys, aged six and four, to visit his parents who lived on the other side of town, in Samanabad. Zaheen could drive and on the days she wanted to do her shopping, he left the car with her and took a taxi or bus to work.

He tried to think of Zaheen's face as she heard from him the story of the strange letter. It surprised him that he couldn't form a picture of her in his head. Was this a sign? Perhaps he shouldn't tell her any of this. Women are suspicious by nature and she might create a mountain out of a molehill. She might think he had done or said something to encourage the writer of this letter to make such an overture. The writing was indeed bold. One might be led to believe that the woman already knew what his response was to be. Just then, as a cloud of dust blew across his windshield while he waited at a red light, Sami reached into his pocket with his left hand, withdrew the letter, crunched it into a ball and threw it out of the window of his car. A gust of wind blew it away.

The second letter arrived on a day when he had been away from the clinic. His father had suffered a mild stroke and he was with him all day at Mayo Hospital. In the evening, just as the evening *azaans* were being relayed from the loudspeakers of the mosques ubiquitously scattered about in the city, he arrived at his clinic. Five or six patients with long-suffering expressions sat in the waiting room, among them a young woman he did not remember having seen before. For a few seconds he paused at the door of his office. His heart missed a beat. He remembered the letter. Rafi, relieved to see the doctor arrive, ran toward him. Sami slammed the door quickly.

With his characteristic persistence Rafi stuck his head through the opening in the door. "Doctor *saab*, the post is on your table and today we have three new patients. Mrs. Niazi's sister is also here. Should I send her in?" Rafi had obviously planned the order of the visits already. Relatives, then friends, acquaintances next followed by their relatives, and finally the others. That was the standard procedure at any doctor's office.

"Just wait a few minutes. I'll ring when I'm ready." Sami picked up the mail. The envelope, the handwriting on it already familiar, peeped from under a newsletter from the Pakistan Medical Association and some correspondence from Pfizer, a drug company. White, small, so different from the rest.

He sat down. Today he was not as nervous. A certain excitement seemed to take hold of him, a feeling of anticipation nibbled at his thoughts. He ripped open the envelope. The same paper, the same dark blue ink, the same neat and ordered handwriting. But the heading had been changed. "My dear Sami *Sahib*," it now said. He was reminded of his adolescent letter. 'Queen of my dreams.' What foolishness.

He became aware of noises in the waiting room. The patients were complaining. He heard Rafi say that Doctor *saab*'s father had been ill, they must show some deference. A solicitous chorus arose. Rafi proceeded with details. He had taken charge.

Sami started reading.

> I have seen you look worried. Is it because of my letter? I do not wish to upset you, to make you feel anxious. My greatest desire is to give you something you do not have. A woman's friendship, her trust, her companionship. Do you not want all of these things? Think of what we can have, together. I will be in your office one day. Of course you will not know me. This secrecy is important because I am placing my honor at stake and I cannot reveal myself until I am sure you want what I do.

Why were women always so preoccupied with notions of friendship and companionship with men? How they liked to complicate their lives by yearning for something they wanted only in principle instead of being grateful for what they actually had: a man to protect them, to take care of them, to give them children. For friendship they had friends, sisters, cousins, that whole noisy lot a man had so little patience with.

This time the letter ended with the words "Yours, Nadira." Yours. The word tickled his heart, his body was suffused with a warmth he had not felt in a long time. What was this! Folding the letter carefully, he slipped it back into the envelope and placed it in his desk drawer, the one he always kept locked.

⋄⇒◉⟨⋄

Sami Ahmed deemed himself a man of integrity. He was also a faithful husband. He had not so much as even looked at another woman with lust in his heart except perhaps some of those American actresses in the movies who made it very difficult for any man to keep his thoughts completely on track. His practice brought him into close contact with women of all ages and all types. Some were young and extremely attractive, some middle-aged and extremely attractive, others not so attractive but very attentive, like Mrs. Niazi, and those other women who wore *burkas* and hid themselves from the world, but thought nothing of lifting their veils in his presence to talk to him about their innermost thoughts and who believed he was as near to God as they would get in this life. Not once had he been tempted, nor had he given any of these women more than professional attention.

At home, he had a good relationship with his wife. There were periods of lovemaking when he wasn't too tired, and he had never imagined that he and his wife didn't have good sex. Zaheen had never complained, but then women don't like to talk much about such things. Anyway, there was nothing to complain about. He was a good husband, was he not? Did he not provide his family with all the comforts they needed? And he didn't embroil himself in scandalous affairs like some men he knew, like his best friend Hanif, for example, who had been seeing a married woman for three years and was now on the verge of breaking the news to his wife. Sami suspected she already knew and had no choice but to remain silent, for the sake of the children of course.

And so, being the man he was, Sami was agitated by the letters. What made matters worse was the knowledge that he experienced what he guiltily recognized to be an unwholesome excitement from this curious correspondence. The woman (if she was that and not a man pretending to be a woman and out to dishonor the doctor for some imagined grievance) had not suggested a meeting as yet nor had she offered to speak to him on the phone. But he knew, the agitation growing to disturbing proportions, that a phone call would come soon. Such was the nature of life in the city. Letters belonged to an older, slower time. Now it was the telephone, that instrument of immediate gratification, which generated communication. This knowledge brought in its wake further trepidation. What if she chose to call at home? He remembered a cousin whose wife left him simply because a strange woman who never disclosed her identity kept calling her to offer details of a sordid romance involving her husband. The couple began to quarrel. Ugly scenes ensued. She accused him of infidelity. He protested, violently, and before long they were throwing things at each other and one day a side table he had flung at her struck her on the side of her forehead and she fainted. The children, a boy only seven, and a girl nearly ten, ran out of the house in terror. The father went after them and dragged them home only to find his wife bleeding from the spot that had received the impact of the chair. She had to be hospitalized. In a month a divorce followed. The whole family was torn apart.

Sami shuddered as the details of that unhappy, miserable incident returned to him. His wife must never know of the letters. He must destroy the one in his drawer the very next morning. Having made that resolve, he found himself wondering, somewhat foolishly, when the third letter would be coming and what it would say. That night Sami tossed and turned in bed with no peace in his heart.

"Are you all right?" Zaheen asked him. "Are you worried about Abba?" Her voice was tinged with sympathy.

He was suddenly, ashamedly, relieved that he could respond hastily with "Yes, I am worried. A stroke, under the best of circumstances, is a horrible thing, and he's old and so weak." How easily the lie came to him, he thought as he shut his eyes and beckoned sleep to come to him.

The next day the phone call arrived just as he had finished prescribing antibiotics to his last patient. Rafi informed him irately that it was some *'Begum saab'* who didn't want to speak to the receptionist but wanted only to speak to 'Doctor *saab.*' His patient, an older man who had bronchitis and looked frail and helpless, fumbled as he folded the prescription that had been handed to him, slipped it into his front coat pocket, and touching his forehead in a *salaam*, left the room.

Sami picked up the receiver and feigned a disinterested "Hallo."

"Hallo." The voice did not sound familiar. Sami was not given to easily recognizing people's voices on the phone. Always, he was too distracted, his mind was elsewhere, so that unless the voice at the other end identified itself, he failed to connect it to anyone he knew.

"*Salaamalekum.*"

"*Walekumsalaam.* Who is this?" He bravely maintained a wooden inflection. Inside his chest his heart rocked as if it were a boat cast on turbulent waters.

"It's me." The voice quivered. Sami could picture a smile, a slight curling of the lips.

"Who is this please? I'm very busy today. Is it Mrs. Niazi?" Sami attempted to sound brusque.

"No, you know it's not Mrs. Niazi, it's Nadira. Can you talk?"

"Look, I don't know any Nadira and if you are sick please make an appointment with the receptionist." He felt he had taken charge.

"Of course you know me." The voice was smooth, a little husky, perhaps because she was speaking in a hushed voice. Sometimes she spoke English and once in a while she lapsed into Urdu.

"What do you want?" The words fell out of his mouth without his volition. He sat back in his chair and looked straight at the door of his office, noticing that the paint was peeling in one corner, wondering foolishly at that moment if Rafi could hear him.

"I want only to be with you. But what do you want?"

"I don't want anything. This is not proper. Writing to me and calling me like this is not proper at all. You know I'm married, I'm happily married, so why bother with me, hunh?" He decided the direct approach would be the best.

"If you're so happy why do you sit here in the office, long after the last patient's gone?"

"I stay in the office to read. Reading at home is difficult . . . anyway, it has nothing to do with being happy or not being happy. But what you are suggesting is impossible. I want to tell you right away I will not be drawn into this trap you're trying to plan for me. Please don't call here again and please don't write." He injected his tone with as much disapproval as he could muster. He also raised his voice a little. After this he should have banged the receiver down. Instead he kept it to his ear. There was silence for a few seconds at the other end.

"How much better if we sat across from each other and had this conversation. Then you could see I was not out to trap you. You would see I was sincere." His show of anger had not produced the desired effect. She did not appear to be ruffled by either his words or his tone. Her persistence proved unnerving.

"Look," Sami erupted impatiently, aware with a sick feeling that he should end this conversation before it went further, "I don't know what it will take for you to understand that what you want is impossible. However . . . " What was he doing? The voice of caution reared its head. Stop! "If you have a problem that you wish to discuss, come to the office. You obviously know the clinic hours. Make an appointment with my receptionist. . . "

"Can I come now?" She cut him short. He imagined the smile becoming coquettish. His heart raced.

A glance at his watch showed it was past nine already. Rafi was closing up the office. The receptionist would come in with the next day's appointments and she and Rafi would leave together in another ten minutes.

"No, I will be leaving soon. If you wish to see me come tomorrow around one. Rafi, my attendant, will show you in. Tell him . . . tell him you're my wife's cousin." The words slipped out without effort.

She didn't say anything. There was a click and she was gone. Sami replaced the receiver on the cradle. His hands were clammy, even though it was mid-December and tonight was particularly chilly. Would she come?

⋆⇀═◉═⇀⋆

She didn't come, or if she was among the five or six new female patients he had that week, she didn't reveal herself nor could he guess if it was one or the other. In his heart he suspected that she was one of them. For a while the tall, slim woman who complained of stomach pains, whose fingers were long and bare of rings, whose eyes were thickly edged with sooty-black lashes, whose full, red lips curved in a bashful smile when she presented her symptoms, and who was wearing some kind of a perfume that seemed to insinuate itself in his brain and excite his thoughts, seemed to be the one. She glanced at him sideways, as if she couldn't raise her eyes and look at him squarely. As he listened to her complaints he felt a familiar warmth creeping up along his thighs. His chest constricted with some emotion he could not name.

"Doctor *saab*, I have these shooting pains," she said in English, the voice trained at an English-medium school. "They start from here," she pointed to the lower left side of her abdomen, "and go up all along my arm." There was such detachment in her eyes, they were so devoid of anything except a concern for the shooting pains that Sami cursed himself for his stupidity and, feeling once again as if he were the boy with the kite string slipping from his hands again, he adjusted the knobs of the stethoscope in his ears and bent forward attentively.

At night, unable to sleep, he picked up a medical journal from his bedside table and started flipping through it. "Risk Determinants in Survivors of Myocardial Infarction" caught his eye and he told himself he should read it. Zaheen was putting the boys to bed. He could hear her talking to them in the low, hushed voice she reserved for bedtime conversations with them. With a feeling of dismay he realized he didn't know what she said to them as she tucked them in. Did she tell them stories? Did she read to them from story books or did she tell them the old tales that were handed down orally from one generation to another? The story of the flea that greedily downed a whole stream and suffered from catastrophic indigestion, the parrot that could never keep a secret, the princess who lived in the flower of the pomegranate fruit and waited eternally for her prince. Perhaps she read to them. With a twinge of guilt he realized he had never seen the story books in his children's room. When was the last time he was there?

The phone rang with a loud, jarring sound and he jumped. The journal slipped from his hands and fell off the bed and his mouth became dry.

He fumbled with the receiver. "Hallo," he croaked.

"Doctor *saab*, *salaamalekum*, it's Jamal Syed. My wife is complaining of severe pain in her right leg, she's unable to sleep." The husband's voice sounded troubled, apprehensive.

Swept over by a wave of relief that almost took his breath away, Sami transferred the receiver to his other hand and lifted himself on his elbow. "Does it come and go, Jamal *sahib*, or is it continuous?" Calming his nerves, he assumed his professional tone.

Jamal spoke to his wife. Sami heard the sick woman's voice in the background. "Doctor *saab*," Jamal continued, "she says it starts whenever she moves her leg and it spreads all along the side, she's in terrible discomfort."

Sciatica. Can't do much about it. "She should rest, avoid sudden movements and tomorrow I'll see her in the clinic. It's not serious." Sami comforted the distraught husband.

When Zaheen returned to the room he was lying on his side with his eyes closed. Phone calls were normal at any time of the night in a doctor's house, but he was stricken with the thought that Zaheen might ask who it was and he would then be forced to talk to her. He didn't wish to talk to her. There was too much on his mind.

She moved under the covers unhurriedly, sighing gently. Why was she sighing? Was something wrong? Did she suspect anything? How could she, unless . . . His heart lurched. Zaheen sighed again and turned so husband and wife lay back to back, facing away from each other. Sleep evaded him; like a kite caught in sudden strong wind, tugging, pulling, it ran from him.

The sun was just a dash of orange on a shadowy horizon when he awoke the next morning. For a few minutes he stared at the sky through the gap between the window curtains, seized with a strangeness he couldn't account for. He felt as if he was someone else, not the man he was yesterday or the day before that, a man who should not be in this bed, in this room. The clock on his nightstand said 6:30. In another half hour Zaheen would be up. Slowly he slipped out of bed. For a few seconds he stood still, not sure of what it was that he wanted to do. Ignoring the impulse to return to a warm bed he left the room and walked over to the boys' bedroom.

The children were sleeping soundly. He could hear the soft, rhythmic murmur of their breathing. The room looked different. The beds were new and Zaheen had put up framed pictures on the walls, animals and scenery, prints she must have cut out of calendars. A small white bookcase held the boys' store of books. Sami bent down to examine them, fingering the spines while he peered at the titles. As his gaze traveled lower he observed that the second shelf contained books that were not children's books at all. *Jane Eyre, Lady Chatterley's Lover, Wuthering Heights, Rebecca, Gone with the Wind, Pride and Prejudice,* and Urdu novels as well, *Dastak na do, Terhi Lakir,* other titles not so familiar, also newer works in English perhaps by American and British authors. These were Zaheen's books. She had been reading.

Sami was surprised. Why, he didn't know. After all, Zaheen was a well-educated woman. She had a B.A. from Kinnaird College, one of the most prestigious colleges for women in Lahore, she spoke English fluently, and she also had once been fond of painting. Sami remembered how taken he was with the fact that his wife-to-be was so talented. Some of the paintings she had done before she was married now hung in their drawing room and their bedroom. One, a still life with roses in a vase and books had been Sami's favorite in the days he was engaged to her. He couldn't remember why she had stopped painting. Of course. The children, she said once. They would get into the tubes of paint no matter where she set up her easel.

After some thought he realized he was surprised to see the books because he had never had occasion to find Zaheen sitting with a book propped in her lap. Always she was running around the house, doing this or that. Maybe she also read the newspaper after he left for work.

He tiptoed back into bed just when Zaheen was stirring.

Suddenly, just as he had anticipated, the letters stopped. Instead, Nadira now called him regularly, every night soon after he had finished with his last patient. It was as if she had a clairvoyant view of how many patients he had and when he was seeing the last one. After the third telephone call he sent off Rafi and the receptionist, telling them he would lock up himself. "I have some reading to do," he told them, pointing to a pile of journals on his desk. Rafi, the conscientious caretaker that he was, exhibited reluctance to let the doctor do what he had been doing himself for five years. "But Doctor *saab,* I'll stay as long as you want, I'll take care of it, don't worry," he said in a worried tone. Sami persuaded him it was all right, he should go and not worry. The pile of journals on the doctor's desk grew and Rafi finally realized his employer meant business.

Tonight, when the phone rang he was alone in the office, riffling idly through *Cardiology Updates,* having paused at "Anthracyclines and the Heart" several times with the intent of reading it.

"Were you waiting for my call?" Nadira asked with a quick laugh. There was something about the manner in which the tiny laugh came at the end of a word quickly, almost as a part of it, that made it sound familiar, as if he heard it every day. But, despite all his efforts, he was hard pressed to link it to anyone he knew.

"Yes, I was. But I don't have much time. Yesterday I got home at ten-thirty and if this continues, Zaheen . . . my wife will know something is wrong." So now he was plotting to deceive his wife.

"Perhaps she doesn't really care. After all, you're a doctor, doctors have emergencies and can be held up by sick patients without any notice."

"Yes, that's true. But still . . . anyway, when are you coming to see me? Are you going to be a mystery woman forever?" Sami heard her laugh in response to his daring query. Was she laughing at him?

"Soon, be patient. So how was your day today?"

"It was all right. The same old routine, nothing different."

"Are you bored with your work?"

"I used to find it exciting, but now it's just all the same. There's no challenge in seeing patients suffering from the flu, from pains and aches, from diarrhea, men and women who seem to court sickness just so they can have some change in their lives." Why was he telling her all this? He had never even admitted any of this to himself. Not once had he openly admitted that he missed the excitement and challenge of real medicine. Diseases with long, complex names sprang at him from his journals, and he read about them as if they were exotic tales from faraway lands, with avid eagerness and hunger. He envied doctors who made life and death decisions, who pulled despairing patients out of the darkness of death and hopelessness, who walked around with a swagger, arrogantly. Set aside for him seemed to be the commonplace—flu, skin rashes, diarrhea, aches and pains—illnesses that often needed no more than placebos and pep talk to evince a cure.

"Why don't you do something about it?"

"Like what? Life is a drudge, I have to make money, the family has to be provided for, and there's no other choice, is there?"

"Isn't there?" Nadira's query was like herself. A distant, mysterious, enigmatic suggestion.

They talked, he more than she, and when he closed up the office it was nearly ten-thirty. He should have called Zaheen to tell her he had been held up.

She opened the door for him when he rang the doorbell. The houseboy was nowhere in sight. Perhaps he was already asleep. It was past eleven. Sami began mumbling about a troublesome patient, keeping his eyes away from Zaheen's face as he recounted the problems the patient was having. Zaheen listened without amazement, nor did she complain about the lateness of the hour, which surprised him. Was she going to be surly because he was late?

"And the traffic, even this late, was awful. I don't understand where people are off to at this hour of night." He grumbled, irked by her silence.

"Well, those who work late have only this time for some recreation," Zaheen said, making her way to the kitchen. "Not everyone is eager to get home and to bed," she added with a cheerful smile. So, she wasn't angry. Relief flooded over him.

The next morning Sami felt he was coming down with a cold. The hazards of his profession. A cold was such a nasty business, especially for a doctor, especially when one could do little about a perpetually runny nose and sniffles. To his patients he'd say, take two aspirins, inhale some steam, drink lots of liquids, and keep warm. To himself he said none of those things, because nothing helped. Only time took care of the common cold. Everything else was a well-intended deception. He called the office, told Rafi to cancel the morning patients and gave orders that if someone seriously ill put in a call to the office, he was to be contacted at home at once.

Zaheen was still in the kitchen. The boys had left for school. Sami showered, standing a long time under the hot water, letting the steaming warmth seep into every pore of his body. His eyes were closed and his head was filled with reflections of Nadira and when he would see her and how she would look. Suddenly he was gripped with a fearful thought. It was as if the water had been turned off suddenly and he had been doused with an icy cold splash. What if she was an ugly hag of a woman? He froze. Steeped in the vanity of his own desire, he had not thought for a second that Nadira was anything but beautiful and young. Like his rooftop beloved. Unable to shrug the thought away, he shut off the water and came out of the shower quickly. As he rubbed himself with a towel the image of a woman unlike any of the pictures he had formed in his mind of Nadira arose like a specter before him. Could that soft-textured, sugary, teasing voice belong to anyone whose face was not like the moon? Yes, it could. And she might also be fat, like Mrs. Niazi, whose voice was soft and sugary as well. What had he done!

Sami sat down on his bed as if someone dear to him had just died. He shivered and his nose began to run. Within minutes he was sneezing. He stood up, restless and anguished by what was now passing through his head. Perhaps she was Mrs. Niazi, after all. Oh God, no! His eyes burned and brimmed over as his nose filled up again. He looked for the box of tissues Zaheen kept on her dresser. It wasn't there. Opening the top drawer of his wife's dresser, he searched for and found another box. As he was struggling with a Kleenex his glance fell on a sketch pad lying among Zaheen's toiletries. Was she sketching again? And what was the pad doing here, in this drawer, nestled among Zaheen's cosmetics, her ornate jewelry box, her hair clips and combs, her hair brushes? Sami removed the pad out of the drawer and lifted the cover. A pencil portrait of their younger son, Arif, stared at him. Had she been practicing? The drawing was good, well-executed, a faithful resemblance. He turned over the page. A blank page. But his eyes fell on something stuck to the white emptiness of the thick grainy paper that he thought at first was an illusion. No, not that, something else. Perhaps Zaheen was preparing to create a collage.

He was wrong. What he saw was no illusion, no collage. It just sat there, as if it were meant to be there, snug, unmoving, still. An ordinary white envelope, harmless in its appearance, so familiar. His heart missed a beat. So misery had already crossed his doorstep. What did this letter say? Why had Nadira betrayed him? How long had Zaheen known? Why hadn't she said something last night? What was she waiting for? Why had fate played this trick on him? The questions buzzed in his ears as if they were harsh, cacophonous voices.

Just as he had lifted the envelope from its place of hiding he heard footsteps behind him. Turning, he saw Zaheen standing in the doorway. Their eyes met. The envelope fluttered to the floor from his hand like the last eddying leaf broken off from a bare-limbed, autumn tree. He noted that a look of astonishment spread over her face like a slow blush. So, she had not planned on telling him about the letter. Why? He was puzzled.

She made no attempt to move. One hand firmly on the doorknob, she returned his gaze silently, without flinching, her face suddenly pale, her eyes brimming with tears of accusation.

First published in *The Toronto Review of Contemporary Writing Abroad*, vol. 15 no. 1, Summer 1996.

⟶ Atonement (Lahore Diary) ⟵

March 14

My mother, who is seventy-five and has glaucoma in both eyes, is riveted to the television screen. She is leaning forward in her chair, her frail, bent body restive, her hands fidgeting with the *dupatta* that keeps falling off her shoulder. Finally she lets it collapse into her lap. Her left hand comes to rest under her chin, with the right she caresses her painful knee joint. Not once do her eyes stray from the TV screen. Every now and then she mutters something under her breath, the sounds she makes reminiscent of the time when we were children and had done something to incur her displeasure.

She is watching the 1996 Cricket World Cup.

And so is everyone else in Lahore, I think, except me, because I'm visiting from another continent and also because I despise all sports. There's more. I also have difficulty pretending the cricket match between Pakistan and India is really war. My mother, on the other hand, feels absolute certainty on that score. And because it's war of course we must win. "*Ham jeetain ge*" (We shall win), a song especially created for the occasion proclaims in loud frenzied refrains during commercial breaks. We are a passionate people. I shudder to think of what might happen if we lose the match.

As I sit next to my mother and look at the cricketers in the field I cannot tell who's Pakistani and who's Indian. Sooner or later I will have to identify uniforms. For my mother's sake I must make an attempt to know what's going on, occasionally I too must grunt in ire or howl with pleasure and sing along with the others when "*Ham jeetain ge*" comes on. Already she isn't too happy with the news of my short stay this time. And being critical of the scene before me will further incriminate me in her eyes. So I keep my mouth shut and feign interest.

March 15

Another song, not fervidly patriotic, but passionate nevertheless, has taken the nation by storm. It's Pakistani rap, I'm told, and when I hear it I'm quite taken with its wild rhythmic beat and the Punjabi lyrics which are an unusual mix of snatches from old folk songs. But the first line is what the people are astir about. *"Assan te jana ai Billo de ghar/ Ticket katao, lain banao. . . "* (We are going to Billo's house/Let's get tickets, let's get in line). Fights have broken out in the city because of it. Proud young men who would lay down their lives to preserve the honor of their womenfolk are up in arms because they see in the song insinuations intended for their Billos. The lyricist should not have chosen a name that was so common among women. Why, everyone thinks it's their Billo! I know at least two, one in my own family, a cousin.

And before we know it, despite sales that will make the creator of the song a millionaire by year's end, there have been public condemnations. Indeed, we are told, this is cultural obscenity, unfit for an Islamic nation. The nation is swayed this way and that. Cricket is momentarily forgotten as crowds attack a theater where the performers had been interrupted before they could sing the Billo song. Angry and disappointed, the crowds demand that the song be sung as scheduled. We are a people easily riled and not easily appeased. Our fervor for cricket is matched only by our penchant for folk music.

But soon the match rises above everything, like rain clouds sweeping over a dry, white horizon, darkening the atmosphere, filling hearts with exhilaration at the promise of rain. All else is forgotten. Once more my mother and the others in her house station themselves before the television set. I have waited all day to talk to Amma of the place across the seas I call home, of my new job, of my husband's diabetes and my migraines, but she has been too busy. In the morning the house had to be cleaned, the wash sent out to the laundry, yogurt for my father's breakfast *lassi* had to be curdled. And then, when all of that was finished, I followed her as if I were a little girl again, asking for this, for that, being a pest. We sat down for a while, but she had more to say than I. I listened. Now the match has started and I must wait. The cook is here too now, in the TV lounge, and no one knows what we will have for supper tonight. Perhaps it will be *seekh kababs* and naans from the main market again.

Today I know the uniforms. The Indians are wearing blue and the Pakistani players are in green. The color of Islam. Also of spring and hope. I preferred the crisp, white uniforms of the earlier cricket seasons. There was something innocent and naive about the game then, a graciousness that we seem to have lost. Something else has taken its place, something insidious, nameless, without form.

The gradual realization that all the Pakistani players have mustaches, while only a few of the Indian cricketers sport the bushy appendage assists in keeping track of who is who. Some of the play terminology too has become comprehensible by now. Overs and wickets are beginning to make sense. I know for example that when the wickets fall it's all over. But this over isn't what the other over is; I'm surprised to discover that an over is a series of six balls bowled from one end of the pitch. The pitch, of course, is the playing area. As for the bowlers and batsmen, they are men of distinctive and separate artistry. I remember that many years ago a cleric condemned a bowler because he had developed the habit of rubbing the ball against his thigh before making a throw. An obscene gesture, we were told grimly by men who knew about such things.

My mind wanders. I've been browsing through today's newspaper and scattered reports about more killing in Karachi catch my eye. The headings inform casually, as if death in Karachi is an everyday occurrence, to be expected, banal. But it is, I tell myself, an everyday occurrence, and to be expected. So what? we ask ourselves, and when will it stop, the killing, we demand to know, the question reduced to rhetoric. There's a picture of a thin, hollow-eyed woman with a heavily lined face whose mouth is open in a scream of despair. Her son, a fifteen-year-old schoolboy, has been shot through the head. Far from home, on his way to school, he was caught in a crossfire. She cradles his limp body in her arms. Other women around her look down at her, their faces mapped with grief, their lips distorted in anguished cries. There are other stories as well. About torture cells, about abductions, about police brutality, about the woman whom people refer to as BB, the woman who failed at leadership. There's news of cricket too.

I turn from the newspaper. The excitement in the room compels. Half an hour into the game I find myself occasionally slipping to the edge of my seat, my fingers tugging nervously at a loose strand of hair, the words of the victory song sitting on my tongue like an unwanted guest in one's house. "*Ham jeetain ge. . .* "

A sudden roar startles me. Wasim Akram has hit a sixer. Amma is laughing. How like a young girl she looks when she laughs, I think, the sullenness from the ever-drooping mouth dissipated, the sunken eyes lit up momentarily. How rarely she laughs now. I drop the paper and clap.

In my ears my own shout sounds like an echo of another voice. "Well done!" I'm saying, "Wow!" I too howl with pleasure. The strains of the song build up to a crescendo, the drums beating with a deafening roar.

March 16

Wasim Akram is sick. He's not playing in the last innings and everyone is distraught. What if we lose to India? The thought galvanizes us and also makes us weak with trepidation. Collectively Wasim Akram is cursed and made the recipient of blights. People reminisce with great sadness about the beloved cricketer Imran Khan who would have died in the pitch rather than stay away simply because he was sick. Even if he were weak with a raging fever and couldn't hold himself straight, he would still be out there, giving the game his all. But unfortunately, everyone sighs and swears, one man is not like the other.

The play continues without its lead player and we grip the arms of our chairs in dread. I try to follow the action, whatever little of it there is. Suddenly everyone in the room screams. I realize very quickly these are not screams of joy or exultation. There are groans, Amma is on the edge of her seat, her muttering now audible. She is swearing, her face contorted, her hand extended toward the television screen in a gesture of disgust. Everyone is standing, a young cousin brandishes a fist at the screen, another, a few years older, is rooted to the ground, his eyes fixed in a stare of disbelief. Soon it becomes apparent that we have lost the match. "Ashes and dust we'll win," my mother says sarcastically as the strains of *"Ham jeetain ge"* momentarily echo in the background with a hollow sound.

March 17

The people are enraged. The Pakistani cricket team has to switch to an earlier flight from India in order to avoid a confrontation at home. But the airport is crowded with booing protestors when the plane lands. Later it is reported that the other passengers on the plane shouted and jeered at the cricketers who were secretly escorted under strict security through the VIP gate and then whisked out of the airport in two cars. Newspapers show pictures of women holding up their shoes to the team. According to BBC the team members were abused and pushed on arrival at Karachi airport. And that's not all. Wasim Akram returns home to find it has been pelted with eggs and tomatoes. His mother, fearful of her life, has taken refuge at a relative's house.

Certain reports indicate that the entire cricket team was weeping when it lost. At home, threats have begun to pound at Wasim Akram's door. There are those who would kill him. A young man in Sheikhupura has sent the team bangles, while another young man in Mardan first sprays the TV screen with bullets from a Kalashnikov after he sees his team lose, and then turns the gun on himself. A man who had bet one *lakh* rupees on the team's victory suffers a heart attack and dies. Another petitions in the High Court against the players, stating that Wasim Akram was once a poor man but is now a millionaire. In another case in a civil court Wasim and the head of the Pakistani cricket team have been sued for one *crore* rupees.

"They are traitors," Amma says. "Now Indians will celebrate and make us look stupid."

"I hope they lose too," a cousin adds with vehemence.

"And then we'll celebrate," his younger brother says gleefully, his eyes gleaming with an emotion that could only be envy.

Secretly I too find myself wishing that India suffers a defeat at the hands of Sri Lanka.

March 18

Someone in parliament has announced that our team lost due to the ungodliness of the People's Party; if the Pakistan World Cup song "*Ham jeetain ge*" had used the word *Inshallah* (God willing) after it, it would not be suffering such humiliation today. A cleric says that the country has been punished for its arrogance and its depravity, for arranging cricket cultural shows that included vulgar dances. "We have lost due to the obscene programs on TV," he asserts. Another claims that it is still not too late; the government should perform an act of atonement. The newspaper *The Daily Jang* is claiming that songs on TV such as "*Ham jeetain ge*" stirred the nation's emotions to a pitch. People have demanded that the team members be stripped of their citizenship, that Wasim Akram should wear his earring in his nose. Some people have called the *Jang* office and threatened to blow up the team members. There are also plans afoot to arrange a mock funeral of the team.

This morning effigies of various team players were burnt. Later a procession of donkeys was taken out against the team. Tonight the shopkeepers have turned off the lights in their shops. The streets of Lahore are plunged in darkness.

March 19

"Asian Tiger Eats India." Sri Lanka wins the match. We come out in the streets of the nation with drums. There are fireworks as we ecstatically dance the *bhangra* and fire shots in the air. We make up other songs, create new rhythms so that *"Ham jeetain ge"* is soon a fogged memory. Everywhere there are shouts of *"Allah-o-Akbar!"*

At my mother's house too there is jubilation. Amma and I talk of nothing but cricket. Together we curse, we swear and we exult. She has made *halwa* for me today, the farina browned to a rich gold, specked with almonds laid about like beads of light. The aroma of cardamom fills my mouth as I eat the first spoonful. Amma places more in my plate. "Eat, eat," she urges, her face illuminated with a smile.

The papers are splashed with reports of India's humiliation. Our defeat forgotten, we revel in another's victory. Without passion we are nothing, I tell myself. Let Karachi bleed, I say, while we atone for our ungodliness.

Glossary

achha "Yes" (conversational)

azaan Muslim call to prayer

baji honorific prefix for older sister

Basant a festival of spring

begum honorific prefix for women

bhagar sauteed onions or garlic generally served over lentils

bhangra a Punjabi dance

burfi type of sweet

burka an outer garment with veil worn by many Muslim women

chador a wide shawl-like covering worn by women

chana type of lentil

charpai a rope cot

chawani a four-anna coin

crore ten million

daal lentils

darbar court

dervish an ascetic

dhoti a sarong-like wrap worn from the waist by men

dupatta a long scarf worn by women

gharara wide-legged trousers worn by women

ghazal a style of poem popular in Urdu and Persian literature

gulab jamun fried balls of dough immersed in sugary syrup

gulee danda a children's game (tipcat) in which a stick and a small piece of wood are employed

hai "Oh" (conversational)

hain "What?" (conversational)

hukkah a pipe and its apparatus by which tobacco is smoked through water

jharu broom

kaffan burial shroud

kajal   black eye-liner
kalima   the Muslim avowal of faith
kameez   a tunic
karahi gosht   a type of meat dish
kemkhab   type of brocade
khadar   rough cotton
khuda hafiz   "Goodbye" (literally, "God take care of you")
kundan   type of jewelry
kurta   shirt
lakh   a hundred thousand
lassi   sweet or salty yogurt drink
mai   an old woman
maash/masur   variety of lentils
maidan   an open space, like a field
malmal   muslin
massala   spice mixture; *garam massala*, type of hot spice
maulavi   Muslim cleric
mehndi   a pre-wedding celebration
mehr   a settlement on the wife
mullah   Muslim cleric
namaz   prayer
nikah   religious ceremony at time of marriage
paan   betel leaf
pakora   a dumpling made from chick-pea powder
pallu   the part of the sari that goes over the shoulder
paranda   an adornment for braiding hair
parathas   round, flat bread
phupo   Urdu form of address for an aunt
purdah   seclusion from men
roti   flat bread
saab   conversational distortion of 'sahib'
salaamalekum   salutation
sabziwallah   vegetable vendor
sahib/sahiba   male/female honorific suffix
salaam   Muslim salutation
seekh kabab   skewered kababs
shahi tukre   dessert made from bread and milk
shalwar   type of trousers worn by men and women
shariah   religious law
shariat   religious law

sherwani   a long, fitted coat worn by men in India and Pakistan
tabla   a kettle drum
takhti   a wooden tablet covered with a clay wash for children to write on with a reed pen and ink
tasbih   a string of beads, a rosary
tongawallah   a man who drives a *tonga*, a horse-driven carriage
valima   a reception given by the bridegroom's family on the day after the wedding
walekumsalaam   response to the greeting *salaamalekum*

⇢⇒ About the Author ⇐⇠

Originally from Pakistan, **Tahira Naqvi** now lives in the United States with her husband and three sons. She holds an M.A. in psychology from Government College, Lahore, and also an M.S. in English education from Western Connecticut State University, where she has taught English since 1983. Her short stories have been widely anthologized and her translations (from Urdu) of well-known Indian and Pakistani writers have been published in the United States, Europe and Asia. Her second collection of short stories, *Beyond the Walls, Amreeka*, is forthcoming in 1998, and she is working on her first novel.

Attar of Roses comprises tales told with verve and passion that provide glimpses into Pakistani society, from family relationships, marriage, and rites of passage to societal roles and the impact of political change. But the backdrop of Pakistan does not limit their scope. In "Attar of Roses," a schoolmaster's obsession with a woman whose face he never sees, although rooted in the custom of veiling, also exemplifies the universal yearning for the unattainable. Similarly, the young wife in "The Notebook" symbolizes the plight of all women who experience an intellectual awakening while struggling against oppression.

Naqvi weaves together imagery and tone in a way that enables the reader to feel an affinity for a culture that may, at first glance, seem distant and impenetrable. Romantic, humorous, acerbic and vibrant, her stories inform and entertain.